The Tragedy of Being Happy

Pact Press

Published by
Regal House Publishing, LLC, Raleigh 27612

Printed in the United States of America

ISBN -13: 978-1-947548-36-7

Cover design 2019 by Lafayette & Greene,
lafayetteandgreene.com

Regal House Publishing, LLC
https://regalhousepublishing.com
Library of Congress Control Number: 2018953490

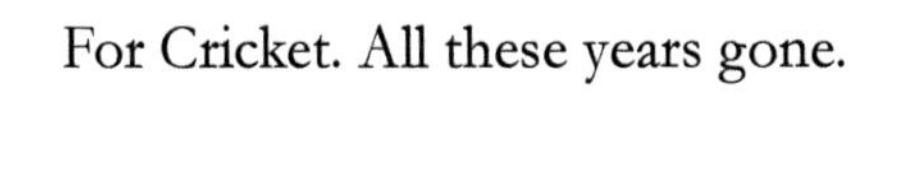

For Cricket. All these years gone.

Part One

Mom brings a man in from the County. Bruce—a massive man with shoulders like a boat's bow, oar-sized hands, and a big head of red hair. I sit on the back porch chain smoking. Starlings gather, a black crowd in the white sky. Thin yellow grass grows in prickling patches. Here and there dirt shows like scabs in the lawn. Dust rises in a small, spinning column.

Bruce talks to Mom. Their voices seep through the screen door. No words, just a reedy noise. Mom's cat stares at me. Once, when I was high, I tried to kill the thing because it was eating my thoughts. Mom stopped me but the cat never forgot or forgave. We have an understanding. A kind of non-aggression pact. It's not love, but then I'm not looking for love.

The door squeals. "Sorry," Bruce says, coming around me. His leg brushes my shoulder. "That looks bad." Gauze wraps my wrist. Blood seeps through it.

"Do you know why I'm here?" he asks. I shrug again. "Your mother's worried."

"Okay."

Bruce lights a cigarette and looks at the sky. I look at the steps and the ants milling around a bit of something in the dust. "Do you think about killing yourself a lot?" Bruce asks.

"What?" I think for a second. "All the time."

"Why?"

"I just do."

"But why?"

"None of it makes sense."

"None of what makes sense?" he asks.

"Everything. I'm just tired."

"You're awfully young to be so tired."

"Old enough."

"We're going to have to do something with you."

"Do something?"

"Yeah."

"Like what?"

Bruce turns away and looks at the mountains. A trickle of sweat runs down the center of my chest. I go to scratch it but change my mind. It doesn't matter. "Are you going to kill me?" I ask. Not that it matters. I'm dying. I know that. Sometimes, the thought of it panics me. Mostly, though, it doesn't seem important.

"Why would I kill you?"

"I don't know."

"I'm not going to kill you."

"Okay."

Long thoughts are hard for me. Things roll around in my head. They bounce and break. They form new thoughts but the thoughts don't last. Ideas and memories mix in a slurry of color and motion. Sometimes, I just feel sick. If I get high enough, things slow down. Just enough to let me think, for a moment, one thought at a time.

"Hap," Bruce says. "What's going on?"

"What?"

"You went away."

"I'm fine." Bruce shakes his head. "Really," I say.

"There's a place," he says, grinding out his cigarette.

"A place?"

"Somewhere safe."

"No."

Bruce sits next to me. He presses his thigh against mine. He leans into me a little, a friendly gesture I don't like. He isn't my friend. He's nothing to me.

"I'm not going anywhere," I say.

"It's not up to you."

I press my palms to my face. "Shit."

Mom packs a bag for me. She packs some clothes. She packs a carton of cigarettes and a book. I sit on the bed. Bruce stays in the living room, making calls.

"You're going to be fine," Mom says.

"Yeah."

She stops and looks at me. "This isn't my fault."

"Okay."

She looks at the ceiling, pale and worn-out. She swallows something thick. When she looks at me, tears cut over the ragged cheekbones. "Look at you," she says. "Look at you." I don't look. Except at the floor. "When is the last time you changed your clothes?" she asks. "Hmm? When? When is the last time you ate? When is the last time you slept through the night?" She swallows the rest of her words. When I finally look up at her, she just shakes her head and goes back to packing for me.

"Okay," I say.

When she finishes, she brings me to the living room.

Bruce stands. "Ready?"

Mom's hand rises. She tries to touch my face. I step away. Mom flinches. She sighs. It doesn't matter. I'm leaving. "I'll visit," she says. "Be good."

"Okay."

Bruce drives an old truck. One with flared fenders and big wheels. Something from the Forties maybe. I don't know anything about cars but this truck is obviously a classic.

Bruce tosses my bag in the bed and opens the door for me. I want to say something nasty about getting my own doors but I don't. I'm tired and it doesn't matter. He comes around and gets in.

"Ready?" he asks. "Seatbelt."

Another nastiness comes to mind. Again, I swallow it. The belt lies tight on my lap and I realize I need to piss. Kind of. Not bad. But a little. I look out the window. Mom stands on the porch, her arms crossed on her chest. Her face is lined and tired-looking, and I decide I can wait.

Bruce drives out of the mountains. Traffic clots the highway. Mt. Hood stands jagged in the east. I smoke and watch the cars. I lean my forehead against the glass and close my eyes.

When I open them again, we're rolling into a parking lot. Evergreens bristle on the ridges. A wide, simple building waits for us in the middle of perfect lawns and trimmed hedges. It's very pretty and controlled. It's vaguely frightening. I sigh.

Bruce looks at me. "It's going to be okay."

"Yeah."

"This is good."

"Really?"

"It is."

"Whatever."

Bruce carries my bag for me. An unneeded kindness. He walks me to the front desk. A woman stares at us with a hard face. Bruce signs me in and waits while I pace. My face catches fire and my hands goes numb. Something hot and heavy opens in the center of my chest.

An old woman comes. Gray hair hangs in thick curls around her shoulders. She smiles when she sees me. A predatory smile. A knowing smile. "Happy O'Neill," she says. "Ready?"

I stop. Everything goes white for a second and the room spins. The floor tilts and I stumble a bit.

Bruce comes and looks at me. He shakes my hand, a little sad, uncomfortable. "Take it easy."

My new room looks over a courtyard with naked trees and brick walls holding ferns and plants. A small seat runs along the base of the window. Two beds, heavy and wooden, lie against opposite walls. Small wooden dressers wait at the ends of the beds.

Half of the room is occupied. The bed's made but the walls are a riot of posters and photos and drawings. Whoever lives here likes their walls busy. It gives me a headache.

Staff searches my bag. She pulls out the socks and jeans and shirts, the book Mom packed—*The Bell Jar*, I think—and the carton of cigarettes. "I'm going to have to take these."

"Why?"

"Policy."

"I can't read?"

"You can get the book back."

"What about my cigarettes?"

"Sorry."

It doesn't matter. Staff finishes pulling my things out of my bag, searching all the pockets. "I need your shoes."

"My shoes?"

"Policy."

"But my shoes?"

"Yep."

"Why?"

"Policy."

I sit on the bed and pull my shoes off. They stink. The woman doesn't even blink. She just takes the shoes and sets them next to the pile of my things. "You wearing a belt?"

I stand and pull it off. I hand it to her. "You can't have my pants."

Staff stuffs my things back in my pack. She starts a litany of rules and gives me a handbook. "Read that," she says. "Everything you need to know is there. Points. Levels. Privileges." I leave it on the little desk and ignore it. "You're a voluntary admit."

"What's that mean?"

"You're here voluntarily."

"But I'm not."

"All you have to do is ask to go home."

"I want to go home."

Frustration fills her face. I can see it in the way her teeth set and the way the muscles jump in her jaw. "I'll have to call your parents."

"Oh. Never mind."

Nothing's voluntary when you're a kid.

❧

"Come on," Staff says. "I'll show you around." I stare at her and she waits. Calmly. Not smiling but not quite unsmiling. My hands form fists. "It's okay," she says. But it isn't. I'm tired and wired. I need a cigarette. "Come on," she says and holds out a hand. I swallow a nastiness and let her lead me out of the room.

C-Ward is long, a single hall the color of cold flesh wrapped around a nurses' station. Wooden doors. Thin industrial carpet. Windows, large and thick with safety glass. Staff brings me to a large room with a ceiling fan. "This is the Commons," she says. Kids look up from the couches along the walls. They smoke and they stare. Their eyes press against me. My face goes to pins and needles. New people bother me.

"This is Happy," Staff says. Someone whispers something. "Be nice," she says. No one says anything. Staff puts her hand on my shoulder. I wince and she flinches. "Sorry," she says.

"Yeah."

She stares at me for a minute. "Dinner in a bit," she says. "Get settled."

"I'm not hungry."

"Try."

Try? Like trying would help.

"Look around," Staff says. "Make friends."

Friends.

"Right."

I walk past my room three times before I find it. Everything's too bright. No shadows. No depth or texture. Everything's smooth and shiny, polished and slick. When I find my door, the plate where the knob should have been is hard and cool.

The room is not empty. A boy stands there. I recognize him from the Commons. He stands naked near the bed closest to the window. My roommate. Poster boy. At home, my room's my room. At home, I have a place to go, a private place, a place where people know better than to bother me. Now, I have a roommate. Something like light flashes in the middle of me. It sticks me to the spot.

The boy turns and frowns. Muscles run long and hard down either side of his spine. Small round scars form vague constellations in his back's brown skin. Magnificent legs drop from an amazing ass. Part of me, the part of me that still appreciates beautiful things, stirs. I have a hard-on. And the boy knows it. His frown stretches into a grin, sly and blistering. "Hey," he says, grabbing a pair of sweats and slipping into them. "You're the new boy." I stuff my hands in my pockets. "What's your name?" he asks.

"What?"

He cinches the drawstring. Scars mar his glorious chest too. "Your name," he says.

I'm suddenly blushy and a bit angry. My hard-on fades, a bit. Feeling comes back to my face. "Happy," I say.

"What kind of name is that?"

Somehow, my feet bring me to my bed. I drop to the

mattress. "When do I get my shit back?"

"Level 2."

"Level 2?"

He smiles. "You'll figure it out."

His waist band dips. A black and thick treasure trail runs from here to there. His eyes. Dark eyes. Almost too dark to be real. Is he doing this on purpose?

"You're dangerous," I say.

That grin again, real this time, moderately goofy, absolutely charming. "Hungry?"

"What?"

He pulls on a sweat shirt. The baggy material covers his glorious chest. It hangs past his waist. Shapeless and institutional gray. All of the beautiful lines disappear. "Dinner."

"I don't eat."

"Everyone eats."

"Shocks the system."

"Serious?"

"Never mind."

He laughs. A wheezing, ragged sound. "Come on," he says. He stops in the door. Part of me wants him to go on without me and part of me wants to follow. "You look like you can use a sandwich."

"Nice."

"True."

I can't help the spreading heat in my belly. I stand.

"Bug," he says.

"What?"

"People call me Bug."

I attempt a smile. It's awkward. I stop. "What kind of name is that?"

Bug drapes an arm over my shoulders. Muscles roll under the bulky sweatshirt, tense and amazing. "The best kind."

We eat in the Commons. Staff brings the food in metal carts. They pull the trays and set them on the tables in the room's center. No one sits at the tables. They get their food and sit on the couches with the trays balanced on their knees. I stand in the door. The room's too full. Too many people move in too many directions. Too many voices talk about too many things.

"Come on," Bug says.

I leave my tray on the table and sit on a hard, blue couch. Bug slumps down next to me.

"Dude," he says. "You got to eat."

I shake my head.

"Unreal," he says.

I'm stuck between Bug and a tall girl with large hair. Her shoulders and her hips command space. She doesn't even try to make room. My skin goes all nettley. Crawling heat and a creeping itch. I do my best to keep still. Instead of scratching, my fingers roll imaginary pills. My tongue strokes my teeth.

"Pudge," she says, grabbing my hand with callused fingers. Bug makes a face.

"Happy."

"No shit?" she asks.

"No shit."

Her laugh is enormous. "Well fuck," she says.

On the room's other side, a boy starts yelling. A ferrety looking boy. Lank brown hair. A chin so narrow it barely exists. Everyone goes quiet and watches.

"You're not listening!" the boy yells, pacing and muttering. His hands wave like fins on a fish maintaining neutral buoyancy. "You have to listen." Staff comes and stands in the door—two men and a woman. "No, I told you…I told you…"

Watching's hard. It's like I can see inside the boy's head. It's like watching people fuck. I don't want to see anymore but the boy keeps talking and walking and I can't stop.

Pudge shakes her head. She doesn't seem to think anything's strange.

"Does he need help?" I ask.

"Absolutely," Bug says.

"What…?"

Pudge leans into me, warm and a little pushy. "It's okay. It's just Curtis. He does that."

Staff walks Curtis out of the room. He goes without fighting, talking to himself and to Staff, and to whomever else whispers in his head, all at the same time. Bug blows smoke rings and breaks them with a finger. Pudge looks at me. Mascara gives her a wide-eyed stare. Uncomfortable to watch.

I look around the room, feeling out of place. People talk. They smoke. They know each other. They're comfortable. I walk out. Bug watches. He says nothing. Not even 'bye. But he watches. He pays attention. That's good. That's nice.

❧

I don't go to my room. My room's not my room. Bug lives there too and I'm just getting used to that. I walk and I walk. The hall's two hundred eleven steps long. I count six hundred steps before giving up. I think broken thoughts. I lose track of myself. My body moves. Things fall away. I feel a little sick. Sweat oozes from me. Nausea rolls just below my ribs. I need a cigarette. I need a drink.

I walk and I think about home. At home, I have a room. Mom works and nights are quiet. Sometimes, someone stops by to get high with me, but most folks stay away. I'm not good with people. People are not good with me.

No one pays me any attention. They go to their rooms and they sit in the hallway. Little groups of noise. Eyes follow me without following me.

A man finds me. "Happy," he says. He's taller than me, blond and so bland I can't begin to guess his age. I stop and blink. "Jim," he says. "I'm your psychiatrist."

"Okay."

"Can we talk?"

I follow him down the hall. He never looks back, assuming I'll follow. Part of me wants to stop, just to see what he'd do. But I don't. A fight this soon seems a bad idea. I have no leverage. Jim's in charge and he knows it.

The room he brings me to is small with a little desk and hard chairs. Boring pastel landscapes hang on two walls, all pale colors and blurred trees, paintings so safe, so mind-numbing that I nearly fall asleep looking at them. I don't want to talk. I want to go home. I want to get high, get drunk.

"You didn't eat," Jim says.

"Shocks the system," I tell him. Jim blinks. "Never mind."

He waits. I wait too. "You have to eat," he says.

"Okay."

"I'm serious."

"Okay." His face goes hard. "Okay," I repeat.

Things get tense for a moment. Jim makes a note on a long yellow pad. Suddenly, I'm exhausted. I need to lie down. Everything gets watery. Swallowing hurts. My throat knots. Everything spins. I'm falling but not falling. I grab my chair with hands that don't belong to me. Jim looks at me. "Happy?"

"Can I…I'm dying."

"You're not dying."

"Really. I'm dying."

"Happy."

I stand. I sit again and I tremble. "Jesus."

"Breathe."

"No…"

"Happy…"

"No!"

Things dip and tilt and spin. Color fades. I puke. I fall. I close my eyes. Only for a moment. The moment goes on and on.

I come out of an absolute and seamless nothing. A heaviness. My body gets lighter and lighter. Banks of white static swirl in my head. I recognize the noises as voices. Something burrows through me, hot and electric. Someone says my name. I open my eyes to a wavering room. I swallow. Gag. I blink. Things clear a little.

A nurse leans over me. "There you are," he says,

unwrapping a blood pressure cuff. "How are you feeling?"

"Crusty," I say, sitting up.

Jim's there. He looks pained. A little pissed. I look away. I push myself to my feet. Vomit slicks my chest and belly. It's slimy and smells viciously of gut.

"Slowly," the nurse says.

"I need a shower."

Jim grunts and shakes his head. The nurse asks if I'm still feeling sick.

"Can I go?"

Jim looks at the nurse and the nurse shrugs. "We'll talk tomorrow," Jim says.

"Right."

I stand for a minute. The room spins a little. I walk with practiced caution. It reminds me a bit of being too drunk, only without the part of getting there.

The shower's wholly inadequate. The water's more warm than hot and it falls in weak streams. A circle of dribbles. Barely strong enough to wash the vomit from my prickling skin. I scrub at myself with a smelly bar of soap. The lines of my body surprise me. Shadows hang deeper between my ribs than I remember. My belly's a bowl. Scars run wrinkled lines in various places, the history of a cutting habit. I find several small bruises on my thigh and spend a long time trying to remember where they'd come from. Nothing comes to me.

Once I'm adequately clean, I turn off the water and step onto the cold floor tiles. A sharp chill grabs my spine. My shoulders and hands quiver. Dressing's harder than it should be.

Bug lies on his bed, reading something, all urgent laziness and grace. I stop in the door. I don't know what to do. This whole roommate thing's awkward. I'm sure there are rules but I don't know them. I don't know how to ask about them. Bug looks up and grins, and I sigh. That grin's charming, disarming, and treacherous. Part of me wants to stare at it forever and part of me wants to run. People scare me. People know things. They do things. Dangerous things. Bug puts his book on the mattress.

"Did you really puke on Preacher Jim?" he asks.

"I guess."

"Seriously?" he asks.

"Not on him, on him."

"But you puked?"

I cross to my bed and lie down. I'm still sick. Weak. Scared. There's no telling what will happen if Bug discovers I can't fight.

"I would've given a nut to see that," he says.

"It's unpleasant."

"No shit." He laughs. "But perfect. Your first day here and you nail the biggest dick in the building. Fucking glorious!"

I curl on my side and breathe through my nose. I try to drag the spinning room to a stop with the power of my mind alone. Unsuccessfully.

"You look like shit."

"Yeah."

Neither of us says anything for a bit. I float out of my body. Things get fuzzy and soft.

"Welcome to C-Ward," Bug says.

They give me something for the nausea and then they give me something for sleep. It's a gentle high. Far gentler than booze but only half as gentle as Oxy. The lines between my body and not-my-body fray. I'm both massive and miniscule. I fill the room but the room's a speck. The walls breathe with me, sighing and bending. I don't want to waste it on sleep.

Slowly, I get out of bed. Perfectly balanced and perfectly easy. My body's not my body and my thoughts are not my thoughts. I'm absolutely empty. Standing's joyous and frightening. For a moment, I think I might vomit again. I stop. I swallow. Once. Twice. I lean against the wall. Things settle.

In the hall, I hear people talking. I hear something that sounds like a television. I hear laughter coming from the Commons. Not in the mood for company, I turn away. I shuffle and sway. Waves roll through me, warm and kind. I feel, for a moment, eternal and divine. Nothing matters.

A girl stops me. She says something but it makes no sense. I stumble. Echoes bounce around my ribcage. They turn the world slightly white. "Hey!" the girl says.

I stop and I blink. A red-headed girl sits on the floor, in a corner at the end of the hall. I'm not entirely sure how I got here and I'm not entirely sure where *here* is. The girl looks up at me and I look down at her. "Sorry," I say. There's something wrong with her eyes. I stare and she stares, and it comes to me. One eye's blue. The other green. "Cool."

She looks away.

"No," I say. She tries to stand. "No. Please." Carefully, I slide down the wall and sit on the floor next to her. She stares at me. Cautious as a cat. I open my mouth but forget what

I'm going to say. My thoughts sway and dance. "C-Ward," I say. She blinks. I swallow.

"What did they give you?" she asks.

"I don't know."

All out of nowhere, details stand out. Red hair but not really red. Gold and brown and even black. The tail end of a bruise under one eye. A scar along a cheekbone's ridge. Another ruining the line of her lip.

"What?" she says.

"What?"

"You're staring."

I blink. I look away. "Sorry."

We sit for a moment. My face itches with embarrassment and my hands hang from wrists that seem entirely too weak and flimsy.

"Jules," she says.

"What?"

"My name."

More blinking. A sigh and a smile. Another flash of heat and, suddenly, I'm stammering. "Hap…"

"Hap?"

Slowly, it dawns on me that this is a chance. A cute girl. A new place. I'm stoned and easy and brave. I swallow again. Not so brave. "Happy," I say. She stares. "Not my fault."

"No," she says.

"My mom…"

"Okay."

It's a moment and the moment passes. Jules closes her eyes.

"What?" I ask. A little shake of her head. "Jules…"

"Go on."

"Did I…?"

She turns and pushes herself to her feet and leaves me there. Alone. Confused. More than a little sad.

For a very long time, I don't move. I sit on the floor in the empty hall and slowly come back to my body. Nausea and pain. Muscle cramps. I shake, sweating a little, feverish. At one point, I stretch out on the floor. The carpet's thin nap bristles against my cheek. Bit by bit, a wet sleep rolls over me. Not a real sleep. A half sleep. A dream-ridden, mixed-up, twisted sleep.

The sounds are so different from home. So many people, so much light and no privacy. I need to get up. I have a room. I have a bed. Someone calls my name. I hear it and try to look but my head isn't attached. My eyes are not my own. They won't open.

"Happy!" A stern voice. "Happy, you need to get up." Hands lift and pull. I bat at them and try to fight, weak and disjointed. More faces and more hands and they get me to my feet and my feet slip around on the floor. "Here we go."

Here we go, I think. *Here we go.*

Sometime during the night, I fall out of my typical semi-sleep into something empty and vast. There's no time or weight or meaning. It's incomprehensible and comforting. I stop being a person and simply wait. No pain or thoughts or nightmares. I've forgotten that sleep can be like this. High, sometimes, I achieve indifference. If I drink enough, I sometimes reach a certain buzzing darkness. This vacant floating's new and blissful.

But then, morning comes. Suddenly and loud. Staff slams through the door, the world crashes into me again. I'm real and solid. I'm nauseated and more than a little confused. Bug groans. "Jesus," he says.

Staff is short and built like a loaf of bread. Big brown hair rolls to her shoulders. A smile too big for sincerity folds her round face. "Morning, boys." Her voice is brassy and far too loud. I roll away and pull the blanket over my head. I don't want to be awake and I don't want to be here. "Breakfast in ten," Staff says. "Up and up."

I pretend for a moment. If I keep my eyes closed long enough, things will go back to normal. I'll be home and I won't have to listen to strangers tell me to do things I don't want to do. For a little bit, I slip back into a haze but it isn't the same. Sounds from the hall. People talk and walk. Doors open and close. Things rattle. Bug groans and kicks his blankets to the floor. "Fuck," he says.

I watch him get out of bed wearing only a pair of scrub pants. No shirt. His back a splendid span of muscle and bone. Beautiful. He pays me no mind and stumbles into the bathroom. He doesn't bother with the door. The shower sings and my imagination takes over. I try to think of something other than Bug but that makes me only think more of Bug. Bug naked. Bug kissing me. My hands on Bug's chest, his shoulders, his ass. Thank God for blankets and walls.

I get slowly out of bed, trembling and weak. A sourness rises from the middle of me into my throat. Everything hurts. Every muscle. Every bone and every joint. My head wobbles on my neck. It's a familiar illness. At home, I'd drink a beer or two, smoke a bowl, pop a pill maybe. Here, nothing but going all the way through the misery step by step.

A nurse stops me in the hall. "Happy," he says. "Let's change that bandage." I stop. I swallow and sway a little. He cocks his head. "You okay?"

I nod and regret it. "Jesus."

"Happy?"

"Okay."

I follow him to the nurses' station and sit in a chair while he unwraps the gauze. Dried blood pulls and the cut opens again, oozing. "This looks a little red," he says.

"Sorry."

He looks at me and frowns. "Maybe the doc should look at it."

"Okay."

"Does it hurt?"

"Now?" I ask.

"Ever?"

I shake my head. Things are settling a bit but not enough.

"Good," he says, cleaning the blood away with sterile water. He tosses the old bandage into a red bucket. "You need to keep it clean. We'll change it again at dinner. It's going to scar."

I don't care about scars. Obviously. Scars run in short runs from elbow to wrist. He can't even see the scars on my legs and belly. My scars. My flesh. My stories.

The nurse wraps fresh gauze around my arm, all the while talking. "Does it itch?" he asks.

"Kind of."

"Don't pick at it. Let it heal." He finishes the dressing.

"Done?" I ask.

He looks at my face and, for a moment, I see judgment there. I see pity and disgust and I want to punch him in his face. I don't though. It's far too soon for that kind of shit. I tuck my chin to my chest.

"Done," the nurse says. I stand, picking at the bandage's edge. He reaches for my hands. "No picking."

I go to breakfast.

The Commons smells of eggs and coffee and cigarettes. Daylight falls through large windows. The Coats Range rises in the distance. Beyond them, home. Blue smoke hangs at head level. My fingertips ache. My hands shake. Shivers creep along my spine.

"Eat," Bug says.

I shake my head. Pudge comes with a plate of biscuits and gravy, bacon and juice. "Fucking keep telling them just cereal and coffee," she says, grabbing a roll of her belly and twisting it hard. It's not much of a roll. Pudge's far from fat but she is big. She's tall and hippy. She has a figure that might turn me on if Bug weren't sitting there. "So soft," she says.

Bug leers. "I like soft."

Pudge winks and slumps down next to us. A vinegary feeling spreads from the center of my chest up into my throat. "Breakfast, Happy," she says.

Bug bites into a sausage link. Dirty thoughts. I droop. "Happy doesn't believe in food," he says.

Pudge stares.

"Shocks the system," I say.

"Dude," Bug says, shaking his head. "What's that even mean?"

He sounds pissed and I don't want him to be pissed. I don't want him to know I don't want him to be pissed so I shrug, all tough and indifferent. "Something I read."

"Bad information," Bug says.

Pudge sticks a piece of bacon in my face. The smell is both repellent and divine. "Bacon," she says. "Everyone loves bacon."

"I'm okay."

She shakes her head. "You're not human."

"No shit."

After breakfast, school. Staff comes in with a bell. The sound of it grates on me. Everyone finishes their breakfasts. They stub out their cigarettes and line up. I'm unused to rules and routines. I don't know what to do. Pudge stands and turns. She holds out a hand.

"Class," she says.

I can't remember the last time I've been to school. School isn't really my thing. I like books. I like reading and, sometimes, I like writing. Not much. Song lyrics. Poems. School, though. Rules. Schedules. People. Everyone thinking they know things. They talk, but they only talk sideways. They take all the gossip and the half-truths and assume they have the whole story. I don't want anything to do with that.

Bug says my name and I look up. Again, those eyes. Dark and wide and so calm. I wonder how he can be so calm. I have to admit, though, I'm kind of curious. Curious to see what comes next. I hate it. But there's nothing else to do and there's Bug, beautiful Bug, and Pudge. What else am I going to do?

Staff waits by the door. Pudge stares at me. I sigh a long sigh and get in line.

"All right, everyone," Staff says. "Let's go."

We walk down the hall. Behind us, the Door to the World. In front of us, another door, identical. Heavy gray metal. A massive lock. No window. We stop and press our backs to the wall. Silent. Staff counts us. It seems silly. I count along, thinking of the Count from *Sesame Street.*

Fourteen! Fourteen crazy teenagers!

No one says anything. I start to get nervous. I'm not good at new things. I die just a little.

To get to the school, we cross a courtyard. A brick path cuts through thick grass. Raised flower beds are filled with color: red and blue, yellow, and lots and lots of green. Small trees with leaves like the hands of tiny children cut the sunlight. Plastic chairs share a patio with a brick barbeque. Bees work here and there. Starlings whirl in the sky. They look a little like blood swirling in water, only black and far more interesting.

The school, a white building, temporary looking, like a trailer maybe, seems to have outlived its usefulness but stumbles on anyway. Again, Staff counts us.

Inside, one room with thin windows. Posters and magazine covers, *Time* mostly, cover the walls. No desks. Tables arranged in a giant U-shape and plastic chairs. Chalkboards hang drab at the end of the room. Waiting for us, the teacher, a big-headed and long-necked man, with a tall wave of black hair and James Dean clothes. He holds his knobbed hands clasped just under his chin, as if watching the most beautiful thing in the world. I don't like him.

Pudge takes my hand. "Sit with me," she says. We find a pair of chairs along one wall, under the windows. Sunlight falls warm on my neck. Still, I shiver. I sit and tell myself everything's all right. No one's going to hurt me. I tell myself there's nothing these people can do to me.

"You okay?" Pudge asks. I'm too busy trying not to scream to answer. Pudge takes my hand. Callused fingertips press into my palm. I look at her and she smiles. "You and me," she says. "We're friends."

The teacher's name is Funk. He waits for everyone to sit before clapping his hands three times, hard enough to bounce tinny echoes from the hard walls. "All right," he says. "Let's begin."

Everyone knows what to do but me. They get up and gather around a table in the corner with boxes of files. They bring workbooks back to their seats and get started on their work. I watch them and I wait.

The room is quiet but not silent. Papers shuffle and pencils scrape. People whisper to each other. The teacher's shoes squeak on the floor as he walks around checking to make sure people are busy. The waiting's heavy. My ribs ache a little. My hands clench. But then he's there, right in front of me.

"You're the new boy," the teacher says. I swallow. "Happy, right? Ninth grade?" He's obviously looking for something. I'm not sure he finds it, but he nods. "Okay." He goes to the table in the corner, gets a workbook and a pencil, and brings them to me. "Let me know if you need help," he says, with a smile. "Just give it a shot," he adds, as if I had already given up.

"Okay," I say.

Numbers, and letters that are supposed to be numbers. Orders of operations and steps to follow. None of it makes any sense to me. School's not my thing and math is my least thing. I struggle and think and the sitting gets to me. I put my head down for just a second. Maybe I doze. Everything turns to bits of sand.

"Hap!" I come back to myself, opening my eyes. Pudge whispers, "Hap. Smoke break." I sit up and stretch. Everyone's lined up at the door. Funk's at the table in the corner grading workbooks. "Come on," Pudge says, pulling at me.

We line up and Staff comes. They count us again. The counting thing's beginning to annoy me. But I keep quiet. I really, really need a cigarette.

Outside, it's the type of day that drags people out of their houses into parks and playgrounds. Hummingbirds, bright and buzzing, chase each other in the hedges. Barbed wire tops a chain-link fence. Music filters through the bramble growing on the far side. Pudge and Bug sit with me. Staff hands out cigarettes.

"So," Bug says. "What's your story?"

"What?"

"Suicide?" he asks. "Voices?"

He's so gorgeous. I want to tell him things. I want him to tell me things. Everything about him turns me on. Trust, though. Not my thing. The world gets very small very fast. This fence is the edge of everything. These chairs and these people are the only thing in the world. Everything else falls away. Even the sunlight seems to come through a barrier of some sort, leaving it thinner than it should be. Colder.

"So?" Bug says.

"What?"

Pudge takes my hand. "Leave him be," she says.

Bug raises one eyebrow. "What?"

Bug's face gets sharp. Pudge looks him full on. "What?" she asks again. This time it's a challenge.

Bug shakes his head. Something's happening and I'm not entirely sure what it is. It's unpleasant. It doesn't matter. I'm not planning on sticking around long enough for it to matter.

They give us just enough time for one cigarette before calling us back to class. The bell again. I'm enjoying being outside. Normally, nature holds no magic for me. I prefer dark rooms. I prefer midnight to morning. But I've been inside a strange building with strange people for the better part of a day now and sitting out in the sun with a cigarette is surprisingly pleasant.

Staff rings the bell, a round, bulging sound. "All right folks," she says. "On the path." Slowly, in small groups, we line up on the brick path outside the classroom again, and again Staff counts us.

"What's with the counting?" I ask.

Bug looks at me like I am stupid and, for a moment, I regret the question. Of all things, I want Bug to like me. I want Bug to think me cool. I want Bug. Period. Even in condescension, he's beautiful.

"Runners," Pudge says.

"Oh."

"It happens," Bug says. "Not a lot, but it happens."

That gets me thinking. I look around at the fence and the brambles. All the doors have big locks and there's Staff, who looks like she might be able to chase down anyone who decides to take off unsupervised. I'm considering options when Staff unlocks the door and school starts again.

Funk stands in the exact same place he had stood when we came in for math with his hands under his chin again. He looks entirely too excited to see us. "Seats, please," he says. "Settle. Focus."

Everyone finds their place. Again, Funk claps for silence and he almost gets it. A boy across the room insists on whispering to the boy next to him. They laugh a little.

Funk waits, glaring with glittery eyes. "Mr. Moreno," he says. Moreno looks up, ready to say something, before changing his mind. He closes his mouth and leans his chin on one hand. "Thank you," Funk says.

He starts in on a lecture about unexamined lives being worthless and worthless lives being unexamined. The whole thing seems stupid and pointless to me. As he talks, he hands out thin books. Poetry. Marvin Bell. *The Book of the Dead Man.* "Live as if you're already dead," Funk says.

Talk turns to living and dying, and the things we think about early in the morning when sleep refuses to let us loose from our worries and wants. We're teens. Our thoughts are mushy and malformed. Funk pushes and pokes. He keeps things from getting too off task.

"Sometimes," one girl says, "I feel like there's no point."

"Nikki," Funk says.

"I'm already dead," she says.

"Let's keep this objective," Funk replies.

"You started it," she says.

"Keep it on the poetry."

"Fear," Moreno says. "Everyone's afraid of dying. If you're already dead there's nothing to fear."

"Bullshit," Pudge says. "There's the dying part. It drains you away. It takes everything you have and grinds it down. You become paste and get spread all around and you stop being you and…and people forget about you. I've seen it. I've seen folks disappear. They go away and they never come back."

Funk's face gets strained. He pinches his lip.

"Dignity," I say. Funk looks at me. "Sorry."

"No," he says. "Go on."

I swallow. Everyone looks at me, waiting. The words seem to fall from my tongue like pebbles without thought. "Dignity," I say. "We live with whatever dignity can gather. We're here and then we're not, and getting from here to there, we have to wrap ourselves in whatever strength we can and take whatever comfort we can. We pretend and we guess and we…we do our best. It's the moment that counts. The never-ending now."

Funk smiles.

"Does that…? Sorry."

"No," he says, nodding. "Good."

Pudge settles her hand on my knee. I look at her. She

winks. On her far side, Bug grins his sly, ominous grin.

❧

Instead of going to lunch, I walk. I ask to walk outside. Even fenced, the courtyard feels bigger than C-Ward's single hall.

"Level four," Staff says. "Only level fours get grounds privileges."

I walk. I drag my fingers along the wall until they go a little numb. Walking helps. Before C-Ward, I walked a lot. I walked empty streets at night. I walked in the early morning. During the day, I slept. Mostly. If I wasn't high, I walked or I slept. I seldom sit still. I am a bit fidgety. Sitting lets things build up. Bad things. Dark thoughts. Suicidal thoughts. Most of the time, I am invisible. Not here. Here, I'm entirely too visible.

So, I walk. Thoughts come and go. Ragged and malformed. Bug's icy prettiness and Pudge's obvious interest are both nice and not nice. Questions with no answers. Hazy plans of escape. Only there's nowhere to go now. These pale walls are a tight fist. Panic flashes, bright and edged. My heart rages against my ribs. The air gets thick, hard to swallow. Too thick to fit in my lungs. I count my steps. One hundred. Two hundred. Three and four hundred.

Sweat trickles down my chest. I'm neither hot nor cold. The air's an industrial nothing. I reach for the pack of cigarettes I always carry in my pocket and find nothing and I remember. I have to ask Staff.

Jules comes and stands in her door. She startles me. "Loud," she says. Those eyes again. Blue and green and wide. They take everything in and give nothing back. No matter how close I get, she seems so far away. Nothing touches her. Not really. She's all collapsed around herself. Nothing escapes. "I don't like loud," she says.

"Me either."

Something about Jules seems hazy. It's as if she's here and not here. In the world, watching, trying to say things but the words get all jumbled and filmy.

"They talk too much," she says, and reaches out a hand and presses it flat to the center of my chest. I flinch. "Are you real?" I step back. "Sorry," she says. Neither of us says anything. But then she smiles a shy smile.

"It's okay," I say. I step back again. "I should…"

"Okay," she says, and turns away. She closes the door.

An achy hollow opens in my middle. My version of hungry. There's food in the Commons. The door's a mouth waiting to swallow me whole. On the other side, people. Food. Light. I go. Step after nervous step. No one notices me. No one stares or whispers. For the first time in forever, I want to be like everyone else.

"Happy!" Pudge unfolds from the couch. She rushes to me. I throw my hands up. "No!" she half shouts. "It's okay. It's okay. Come on. Sit with me."

"I don't…"

"Jesus, Pudge," Bug says. "You're such a hag."

It occurs to me the only reason she likes me is because I'm the newest boy here. Fresh. Pudge likes fresh.

"Fuck you," she says and pulls me across the room.

We fall onto the couch in a bit of a tangle. Bug shakes his head, holding his cigarette over his head, away from flesh and clothes. Pudge reaches up and takes it from him, sucking in a melodramatic mouthful of smoke. I try to unravel myself. Pudge looks panicked.

"Food," I say.

It takes me a second to find my tray. Roast beef. Fingerling potatoes. Bread and Jell-O. My gut hurts a little. I worry about getting sick again. If I'm going to puke, I need something on my stomach to get me through.

After eating, I need to lie down. Too much real food too fast. I'm more used to soup and ramen noodles. My belly bulges and hurts. My head buzzes and my ears ring. Everything dances a little. It's a nasty high without the high part. I don't even stay for my obligatory after-eating cigarette.

"Where you going?" Pudge asks. Her eyes are wide and bright. She reaches for me.

"Sick," I say.

"Oh, sweetie."

"Well, shit," Bug says. "Food does shock the system."

I focused on the door. If I can get through the door, I'll be fine. If I can just get down the hall.

"Do you need help?" Pudge asks.

I shake my head. Bad idea. All the room's edges rush at me then back again.

Shit, I think. *Shit. Shit. Shit.*

"Here," Pudge says, wrapping an arm around me and lifting. "I'll get you home."

If I breathe just right, the nausea stays in my gut. Just right's hard to find though. Too much and my gut swells and hurts and threatens to rise up, all sour and heavy. Not enough and my head gets all swirly blue.

My room's twenty-eight steps down the hall. Twenty-eight immensely long steps. Finally, we get there. The door stands open. I press a hand to the doorframe.

"I'm okay. I can make it."

"No," Pudge says. "You need help." She hauls me to my bed.

"You're not supposed to be here."

She smiles at me. Wrinkles crease between her eyes. I decide to take a shower. Maybe hot water and steam will flush the nastiness out. But Pudge has different ideas. She steers me right to the bed. "Go on," she says. "You'll feel better in a second."

I curl on my side and Pudge strokes my hair. Things go thin and I think strange thoughts, strange words pop out of my muddy brain, bubbles in a geyser.

Feed a fever. Starve a cold.

A good man is hard to find.

A hard man is good to find.

Built like a brick shithouse.

Apparently, I mumble something. Pudge caresses my chin. Her calluses catch on the few whiskers I manage to grow every week. "It's okay," Pudge says. "You're going to be okay." Something about her voice bothers me. It's too soft and too sweet. I tense a little and Pudge snatches her hand away. "Sorry."

I feel bad. Kind of. Sometimes, when people touch me, I think maybe their hands will pass right through me. Pass through my skin and my bones and innards like I'm not really there and, sometimes, I worry I'll disappear.

"Pudge."

Staff stands in the door. This one's new to me. Silver-haired. Old. Maybe fifty. Kindly looking. His bright purple shirt and tight jeans gave him a hippy look.

"Shit," Pudge says. "Sorry."

"Go on," Staff says.

Pudge stands. "I am helping. Hap is sick."

"Go on," Staff says, crossing his arms.

Pudge pouts. "Totally not fair."

"Go."

Finally, Pudge leaves. She takes all the touching with her. For a moment, I just close my eyes.

"Hap," Staff says. "Are you okay?"

"Dizzy."

"Do you need anything?"

"Don't know."

"I'll talk to the nurse," he says. "Get you something."

"Okay."

"I'll be right back."

"Okay."

The nurse gives me something and I take my shower, but the shower's all dribbles and warmish water. Hardly worth the wetness. I sit on the pale tiles, bitter. I like my showers just this side of scalding. I think for a second that I'll never be warm again. Not the warm I want. Not the pink-skinned, loose-jointed warm I crave.

Bug flips the curtain out of his way.

"Hey!"

It's awkward and I think, *Hey. I'm naked. I'm naked and he's right there.*

"You, dude, are so getting laid," he says.

Alarm! Danger! Rushing blood and blinding embarrassment. Bug grins his grin, all knowing and penetrating. Now, far too late and far too slowly, I kill the water. I reach for the towel. Bug hands it to me. Thank God for shock and surprise. At least I don't mortify myself with a hard-on.

"Bug."

"Be careful," he says.

"Careful." Repeating words is a habit. It gives me time to think.

"Pudge," Bug says. "She's not the safest knife in the drawer."

"Seems nice."

"She'll use you up."

I dress as calmly as possible. *Breathe*, I think. *Be calm. Get dressed.*

"Pudge is hot," Bug says, "and she's three kinds of cool, but she'll eat you up if you let her." He picks my shirt up from the floor and hands it to me. Our fingers brush. I keep thinking about how pretty he is. "Your business," he says.

I'm confused. Not sure what's happening or what I'm supposed to do. Bug smiles that smile. I'm beginning to hate that smile.

I decide to take a nap. The bed's hard though and unfamiliar. I lie there and I replay all the touching and the talking. Something busy and antlike marches through me. I float in the space between sleep and no sleep for a long time. Dreams of smoking a cigarette on the porch at home blend with a vision of pigs eating me alive.

Just as I'm about to topple into sleep's endless fall, Staff starts in with that bell again.

"Jesus."

I try to ignore it. I try to hold still, but Staff goes door to door. "Hap," he says. "Group." I get up. Pissed and grumbly.

Group's a circle of hard plastic chairs in a windowless room. Bug winks when I walk in. Pudge grins. A wildly enthusiastic grin. Even Jules is there, staring at a corner up close to the ceiling. Her lips move, silent, distracted.

"Here," Pudge calls, waving at me. She looks half out of her mind with excitement. "Come sit."

A chair stands empty next to her. The only empty chair. I don't want it but what am I going to do? I'm more than a little scared. Small rooms and crowds are among my least favorite things. But here I am and there's nowhere to go.

Staff, a bald old man, a whittled stick of a man trying too hard to appear young, looks up and grins through a silver beard. "Welcome, Happy," he says.

I don't feel welcome. More cornered and pushed than welcome. More crushed.

"Please," Staff says. "Sit."

Moving slowly, I sit next to Pudge.

"You look better," Pudge whispers. "Did you nap? I hope you napped. That's a nice shirt."

Bug shakes his head but the grin's there again. A knowing, I-told-you-so grin. I want to punch him in the mouth. Instead,

I harden my face to indifference, my body to quiet readiness.

Staff clears his throat and everything goes quiet. People slump in their chairs. "Happy," Staff begins. "Why don't you tell us about yourself?"

"What?"

Staff smiles a smile I think he believes is comforting. "Why are you here?" he asks.

"Why am I…what?"

Pudge sneaks her hand into mine. It's cool and a little damp.

"Tell us about yourself," Staff says.

I let the question sit there for a minute. Pudge's fingers squeeze mine.

"What're you afraid of?" Staff asks.

It's a trick. I know it's a trick. He's trying to piss me off, trying to make me mad enough to talk. I bite my lip and Staff stares with eyes so pale you can almost forget they're eyes. Everyone else stares too. They wait. It's too much.

"Listen," I say. "I don't want to be here. My mom decided…I do things. I think things. My mom, she worries. I guess because she loves me. I don't do things like other folks. I do things my way. I don't…you have no idea…Listen, I do what I do. It's my business, it's my life, and I'm getting through…I do my best and now…now, I'm here…whatever. Like I said, I'm here."

I let it sit there for a bit. Pudge squeezes my hand again. Staff stares at me. He's under my skin and he knows he's under my skin and he knows that it's pissing me off. Being a therapist, though, he decides not to push anymore. He got what he wanted. "Welcome," he says.

"Welcome," Pudge whispers.

For the rest of Group, I watch people. I listen to their stories. They tell emotional horror stories. There are tales of rape and other violence. Suicide attempts. They talk about the stress of being different in a world that has no room for different. One girl cries. Pudge stares at me and Bug smirks. Jules is silent and distant. Curtis mutters to himself. At the end, we stand and hold hands.

"One day at a time," Staff says.

"One day at a time," we echo.

Curtis makes for the door like he has someplace to be. The rest of us file out a little slower. I look back. Staff sits next to Jules. Talking. She looks scared. There's nothing I can do so I do nothing.

"Come on," Pudge says, hanging on to my arm.

We walk behind Bug down the hall. I prefer Bug's ass in front of me to Pudge's boob pressing into my arm. Both are nice, but Pudge pushes too hard. She makes me nervous.

Staff lines us up at the Common's door and counts us again, handing out cigarettes to those of us at the right level. Pudge half drags me to a couch. Bug pushes his hip against mine and grins at Pudge's frown. Everyone talks at once.

"So," Bug says. "What brings you to *casa la cuckoo*?"

"What?"

"Show me yours," he says, "and I'll show you mine."

His grin's completely devastating.

"Bug," Pudge says, "leave him alone."

Bug laughs. It seems he's one of those boys who likes

riling people up. The rise he gets from folks turns him on. Turns me on a little too. Physical beauty and mental cruelty. I know he's dangerous but part of me thinks maybe I'll be the one, you know, to save him, to reach that center of sweetness.

"I tried to kill myself," Pudge says, not to be outdone. "Just like you. See?" She holds out an arm. Scars runs from elbow to wrist. Most of them thin and white and not all that serious. One, though, looked like it might have become infected. It's wide and purple and wrinkled like wet paper.

I'm not used to this kind of attention. Mostly, I want people to leave me be. My shit's my shit, but here, in C-Ward, it seems my shit's valuable. A weird kind of currency.

We spend an hour swapping war stories. It's an emotional pissing contest. Lots of *Oh yeah*s and *You think that's bad*s. Each of us trying to convince the others that our hurt's more legitimate, more honest, more deeply felt. Comparing scars isn't really my thing. Pain is private. It's the one thing I'm certain no one can take away. They can add to it but it's always and forever mine.

Still, I end up playing along. I tell them about when I was eleven. My dad died. Suicide. I found the body after school. Mom was working. I told them about the locked doors and having to crawl through the bedroom window. I told them about the running shower and Dad lying in the bathtub, all blue and naked and stiff. The pistol on his belly. The bullet took off the whole back of his head. I told them that I didn't even puke. I did nothing. In my story, I am strong. I did all the right things. The truth, though, was that I sat on the toilet and stared at Dad for a long time, until Mom came home. I don't tell them that. I don't tell them about holding his hand until the paramedics came with the cops to take the body away.

It's already "The Body." Not "Dad." The Body. A memory. An Event.

I don't tell them how I went to bed and stayed there, refusing to eat or do anything for weeks. I couldn't even use the bathroom. For a long time, I pissed in the backyard. I don't tell them that I didn't go to the funeral.

Pudge looks at me with big eyes and I instantly feel like shit. Telling my story's a mistake, a betrayal or something, like I've ruined something pure, something private.

"Are you okay?" Pudge asks, all small voice and kindness. She squeezes my hand and I wonder where the calluses came from.

"Fine." A little surprised that it's almost true.

Until I see Bug's eyes. Bug knows how to use a stare. I look at him and he looks at me. His lips twitch. I stare until I can't stare anymore. I slump back on the couch and close my eyes. I like Bug, in a scary, new way. All I know about love is dim memories of my parents and the occasional fuck for pills or beer. Love, in my world, is all indifference. This oily feeling in my gut's totally beyond me.

I decide that I like Bug. I like, like him. He's gorgeous and he's dangerous. Everything about him is godly. I like that he's fearless and scary, and I like that he has no trouble knowing that I like him. Sometimes, guys get edgy when they find out about me.

Pudge looks from me to Bug and sighs.

"You boys," she whispers. "So, so obvious." She bites my ear. Hard.

❧

Jim calls my name. I look up. He stands in the door obviously choosing not to see what he's seeing. He looks pissed but he doesn't look like he's ready to fight this fight. I stare and he stares back. "Can we talk?" he asks. I get up. Pudge holds onto my hand, stretching out her arm as long as it would go before letting me slip away. Jim frowns. Bug laughs. Something tingles along my spine.

"This way," Jim says, waiting for me to brush by. "Making friends?"

I decide Jim's kind of a dick. "Why do they call you Preacher?"

Jim stumbles a little. But then he catches himself. "Do they?"

"Yeah."

"Interesting."

I swallow a nastiness. Jim doesn't bother looking at me. He takes me to his plain, little office and sits, leaning his forearms on the edge of the table. He laces his fingers and tries to look like he cares but it doesn't work. Jim's face is not made for empathy or sympathy. Too cold. Too set. Like it's only vaguely attached to his head.

"So," he begins. "you look like you feel better."

"I am."

"Nausea?"

"Off and on."

"Muscle pain?"

"Yeah."

"Happy, do you understand what's going on here?"

"You're never going to let me go, are you?"

"You will have choices during your time here, Happy. You can let us help—"

"Help?"

Jim takes a big breath. I realize Jim's bigger than he appears. Not muscular like Bug. Once maybe. But now mostly a memory of fitness. If he were a thousand years younger and less of a dick, I might have liked him. Empty eyes, the color of algae, wait for me to say something. Only I have nothing to say.

"You need to be careful," he says.

"Okay."

He turns his head and looks at me sideways. "You can't afford to let things, or people, distract you."

"Okay."

"There are attractions…temptations," Jim says. "There are people here who will take advantage. Do you pray?" I blink. "I'm serious."

"Okay."

Jim reaches up to his face and scrubs at his nose with his fingertips. I'm getting under his skin. It feels good. I struggle with a grin while Jim fights his face back to bland.

"I spoke to your mother," he says. "She's very concerned." I cross my arms. "She says you cut." He looks at my bandaged arm. I stare at him, not sure what he's looking for, but whatever it is, I'm not going to give it to him. "Why don't you tell me about that?" I raise my eyebrows. "I can't help if you don't talk."

"I don't want your help."

Jim actually smiles. "Irrelevant."

Another nastiness comes to mind. It sticks in my throat.

I look at the ceiling because looking at Jim turns all my thoughts to static. Somehow, a moth has gotten in. It flutters around the long florescent lights, batting and bumping silently. “Moth,” I say. Jim looks up. “Pretty.”

“Happy—”

“The thing about bugs,” I say, “about everything other than us, other than humans, is they live their lives entirely in balance. They eat and they shit and they fuck and they die. They don’t worry about pain. They don’t worry about what other moths think. They are absolutely self-contained.”

“What’re you talking about?” Jim asks, frustrated.

“Never mind.”

“Happy—”

“I’m done.”

“Happy.” I cross my arms. He tries to outwait me. Seconds flip into minutes and the minutes get heavier and heavier. “Fine,” he says.

By the time I make it back to the Commons, it’s empty. No one nowhere. Empty couches. A lonely ping-pong table. The ceiling fan spins, loose and slow. Rhododendrons bloom on the other side of the window. Beyond the rhodies, a lawn, thick and perfect. Green as green ever gets. A tall hedge. Beyond the hedge, I don’t know. A street, maybe. A city. People and freedom. Robins play in the sky. They make me think of what I said to Jim about balance and containment and it makes me wonder if I know what I am talking about.

We line up again and Staff counts us. They hand out cigarettes. Once again, I’m wedged between Pudge and Bug.

Bug acts all cool, as if he's in charge. Like every touch is an accident. As if every time he brushes my arm, it's because he's reaching for the ashtray. As if the pressure of his thigh on mine's because we have no room. Still, the feel of his muscles is warm and wonderful.

Pudge is softer. She stretches, catlike, against the back of the couch. She hooks her leg over mine and lays her head on my shoulder. I'm not used to this much attention. For the most part, people ignore me. For the most part, I'm invisible. Now, though, my world's a whole lot smaller. Suddenly, I'm huge. I'm no longer a speck on God's windshield.

"So," Bug asks, "you got a girlfriend?" Everything about the question's cruel. It's a dig and a game. Pudge goes still and I get cold. I shake my head. "Boyfriend?" Another shake. Pudge leans forward and glares at Bug. He grins at her.

"Do you believe in true love?" Pudge asks. Her face is too close. Her breath smells of bad teeth and cigarette smoke. "What?"

Bug heaves a big sigh. "Jesus."

"Love. Soulmates?"

I shake my head.

"I believe in love," Pudge continues. "People need love. It's the only thing we have that…it separates us from the apes, you know?"

Bug laughs.

"Shut it, you," Pudge says.

Staff saves me from being a chew toy in their little game, bringing the dinner cart in.

"Food!" Pudge gets up and leaves me with Bug.

Bug grins his grin and wraps an arm around my shoulders. "She likes you." He leans in. "I like you too."

"Okay."

Bug tightens his grip around my neck. A little aggressive. A little mean. "Fun," he says. "Right?"

"Yeah. Fun. Right."

I'm not hungry. I don't want to feel sick again. I get up.

"Where you going, sweetie?" Pudge asks. "Not hungry?"

"Bathroom."

I leave the room and stand in the hall. Breathing. Trying to get my skin to stop crawling. I just need space. A little quiet. My heart rolls in my throat. I think maybe I'm having a stroke. I sink to the floor and sit very still for a while, half-hoping, half-dreading.

I sit until the feeling passes, leaving me vaguely disappointed. If I died, I'd be a hero. People always talk about the dead as if they'd done something outrageously brave when they gave up breathing. Especially if they had been young.

I don't die though. I am no hero.

After a while, Staff comes. She invites me to go eat. I shake my head. "We're worried," she says.

"Okay."

"We're talking about putting you on a plan," Staff says. "Do we need to put you on a plan?" I don't know what she's talking about and it doesn't matter. "Jim says you're having a hard time adjusting." I shrug. "It's hard," she says, "I know. But you need to know that we're here to help."

"Okay."

"But you have to help yourself too," she says. "You have to take advantage."

"Okay."

"I'm serious," she insists.

"I know."

"Happy, you need to go eat."

"I will."

"Now," Staff says. She's not going away. She's going to stand there, in the middle of my business, until I get up. So, I get up. "Just try," she says.

In the Commons, Pudge and Bug sit in their usual place. Pudge picks at the chips on Bug's tray.

"Happy!" Pudge nearly screams.

No one even notices, except for Staff, who looks up for a second before going back to his paperwork.

"Dude," Bug says, "you were gone forever. Swimming laps?"

"What?"

"Never mind."

"I missed you," Pudge says, slipping her hand into my lap. "What's going on?"

I look her right in the eye. They're big eyes, dark. Not as dark as Bug's, but dark enough and much, much bigger.

"What do you know about pain?" I ask.

Pudge frowns. "Sweetie…"

I shake my head. "Listen…Listen…"

"Okay."

"My mom sent me here," I say. "She sent me here because I…I'm a black hole, Pudge. Things disappear… You don't understand. You can't."

Pudge reaches up with one hand and cups my chin. I try to push her away but she grabs tight. "I don't care," she says.

"Pudge…"

"Hush," she says. "I don't care."

Bug's hand lands hard on the back of my neck. "Dude," he says, "you think you're the only one with scars?" I look at him and he winks at me. "It's all about the getting there. If you get to the end of the trip with all your fingers, you win."

"I just don't want..." I say. "You don't understand. People get hurt…"

"So?" Bug says.

"I don't want to hurt anyone."

"Fuck you," he says. "My pain is my pain. It's none of your business."

"None of your business," Pudge says.

I look from her to him and then to the floor. "Listen…"

"Fuck you," Pudge says, but she's all grins.

"Guys…"

"Fuck you," they say together.

"Okay."

Pudge leans in and kisses my cheek. "I saved your dinner."

"Okay."

"You need to eat," Bug says.

"Shocks the system."

"Fuck you," they say again.

Part Two

I don't talk to Mom for two weeks. Jim says we need a break. "You need to get used to the routine," he says, "and your mother needs to learn that she can't rescue you."

Not a big deal. Mom and I aren't close. Not since Dad died. Still, Jim's kind of a dick about it. His world, though, his rules. So, I go to School and Group. I take the pills he put me on. Something for the depression and something for the anxiety. Something else for the thoughts I can't stop thinking. They thin things and leave me mushy and weak. I refuse at first, but Jim's all about power. No pills—no points, no smokes, no privileges.

"I'm worried," Jim says, "about your soul."

Jim talks a lot about souls. He talks a lot about "Grace," but his favorite is "Atonement."

"Sin," he says, "is inevitable."

I don't believe in sin but I let him talk.

"Jesus died," Jim says. "His blood washes away our wrongs. There's hope in Jesus. Our God is a loving father."

"Your God," I say.

"Your God, too. Through Him you can be whole."

"Not interested."

Jim's face goes hard. It's like the failure of my faith really bothers him.

"Can I ask you something?" I ask. Something in him lights

up. Maybe he thinks I'm engaging or connecting or whatever. "We're made in God's image?"

"Absolutely."

"And he's without sin?" Jim sees something coming. "But we're...people are naturally sinners?"

"It's a flawed image."

"Flawed?"

"Flawed."

"So, God screwed up?"

"What? No."

"We're God's image, but we're flawed?"

"Free will..."

"Okay."

He stares at me. "Happy—"

"Can I go?"

"Happy, we're not done."

"So much for free will."

On Wednesday, Mom calls. Dinner time. I pick at a bit of meatloaf. I build a small mountain of mashed potatoes. I eat a little. Another Jim power-trip—no food, no points. I stick string beans in the potatoes. Trees of a sort. Pudge and Bug argue poetry.

"Bukowski," Bug says.

"*Blech.*"

"What?"

"I hate Bukowski," Pudge says.

"What's to hate?"

"Casual apathy. Romantic violence."

"Reality," Bug says.

Bug's view of the world is shaded with memories of cigarette burns and fists.

"Carver is so much better," Pudge says.

"He's a drunk," Bug says.

"Dignified," Pudge protests. "He pushed through. He wrote what he saw." She read one of his poems, the one about doctors and cancer.

"Hopelessness. At least Bukowski fights."

"Radical acceptance," Pudge insists.

"Therapy talk."

"Okay," she says. "Olds."

"God!" Bug shouted.

"Are you serious?"

"Periods and babies and shit."

"Women's issues."

"I'm not a woman."

"No," Pudge says, punching Bug in the shoulder. "You're a pussy." He laughs.

"Hands," Staff barks from the door.

Pudge raises her arms. Bug laughs again.

"Hap," Staff says. "Phone call."

Bug and Pudge look at me funny. Calls are rare on C-Ward. We live in our own little world. Nothing exists beyond the walls and fences around us.

Phones creep me out. Something about the distance and the vague feeling that whoever's on the other end of the line might not actually exist.

"Happy," Mom says.

"Hi, Mom."

"Are you okay?"

"Yeah." The line's silent. Not dead but quiet. Except for a small snap and crackle. "Mom?"

"I'm so sorry," she says.

"It's okay."

"No," she says. "Really. I had to do something."

"Mom."

"Okay," she says. "I just...They say I can come on Saturday. Dr. Sweeny..."

"What? Who?"

"Jim," she says. "Dr. Jim. He says I can see you."

"Okay."

"Saturday, then."

"Okay."

"Happy, I miss you."

"Yeah."

"Yeah."

None of it seems real. The voice on the phone is empty. A trick.

"Saturday," Mom says.

"Yeah."

"Yeah."

A coldness opens in the middle of me. An emptiness. Words from English class come to me. *Live like you're already dead.* Dead. Want nothing. Feel nothing. Give nothing. Lose nothing.

Saturday. Staff gives us an extra thirty minutes' sleep.

"Morning, boys," Staff says, his voice almost too gentle to work. We don't move. "Boys, it's time."

"Goddammit," Bug says, tossing angrily in his bed. His feet find the floor.

"Happy," Staff says.

"I'm up."

"Show me." I raise a hand. "Show me more," Staff says.

"Fuck."

"Language."

Groaning, I push myself up and rub at my face. Staff closes the door. Bug stumbles into the bathroom. I get dressed.

"Fucking lovely."

I get my morning pills at the med room, which isn't really a room at all, just an alcove with a pass-through. I stand in line because Curtis gets there before me, and every morning Staff tells him what each pill does.

Curtis has trust issues.

"The Mellaril's for the voices," Staff explains.

"The voices?" Curtis asks.

Curtis has reality issues too.

"I told you," Curtis insists. "The blue ones are poison. You're trying to poison me."

I sigh and Staff sighs. "No poison," she says.

"The blue ones are poison."

"Curtis."

"Poison," he says. "Poison. Poison. Poison."

Curtis has repetition issues.

After I get my meds, I go to the Commons. I get a coffee and Staff gives me a cigarette. I sit in my usual spot on the couch and stare out the window. The sky's lumpy with clouds, waiting to rain but not raining yet. Still yellow and red with the rising sun. My thoughts are slow and thick.

A minute later, Pudge joins me, all made-up like she has someplace to go. Crisp, dark jeans. A blue blouse that make her tits stand out. Her dark hair's a perfect tangle.

"Dahling," she says. "You're absolutely radiant this morning." She kisses both of my cheeks. No one thinks it strange when Pudge goes all movie star. It's part of her charm. She slumps onto the couch and takes my cigarette from me. "Pretty enough to eat."

The flirting's endless and perfect. Part of me hates it. Part of me wallows in the attention. No part of me knows what to do, so I pretend it isn't real.

"Happy Visitation Day," Pudge says.

"Right.. My favorite."

"Sweetie," Pudge says, all concern and compassion.

"I'm okay."

She grabs my hands. Again, those calluses. I turn them over and run my thumb over them. "Cello," she says.

"Cello?"

"Jazz. Some punk."

"Really?"

Pudge laughs. "So sweet. Simple, but sweet." She kisses my cheek. I smell talcum and coffee. I smell hairspray.

Staff brings in breakfast. We eat. Pudge puts down four eggs and five sausages as well as a small stack of French Toast. She downs two glasses of orange juice and three mugs of coffee. It's amazing to watch. "What?" she says, defensive.

I shake my head. She runs her finger through egg yolk and sticks it in her mouth. "I know," she says. "No control. Look at this." She fingers the front of her neck. "Wattle, wattle," she says with a sigh, leaning back into the couch. "No self-respect at all."

"Jesus."

I nibble on crisp toast and poke at a small bowl of grits. I like grits. They don't sit on my gut like eggs or oatmeal. They don't make me all heavy and slow.

Bug joins us, his face still shiny from the shower. He needs to shave. Little black whiskers bristle in patches on his jaw and chin. He gets himself a coffee. He flops on the couch between Pudge and me, squishing us a little and spilling a bit of coffee on my belly. "Sorry." But he doesn't mean it.

Pudge punches him on the shoulder. "You, my friend, are a scrotum wrinkle."

Bug just laughs. He turns to me and grins a grin far too wild for the morning. I scoot aside. His thigh's all hard and wonderful but he's too close. I need a little space.

"Dude," he says, poking me with a fork. "Grits?" He shakes his head and waves a sausage link at me. Dirty thoughts again. I have to turn away to hide the blush. "Protein. You need meat, boy. Real food. Manly food."

I just shake my head and finish my grits.

Just before lunch, Staff rings the bell and people move toward the Door to the World. We're Pavlov's dogs, knowing something's going to happen because something always happens when the bell rings.

I know Pudge's mom as soon as I see her. She and Pudge

look so much alike, it frightens me. They wear identical outfits. Same color. Same cut. Same size. They do their hair in the same way and wear the same makeup the same way. They hug and they squeal. It's hard to see who's the mom and who's the kid.

Bug stops me in the hall. "Happy. This is my mom, Nadine. Mom, Happy." She's a tall woman with thick black hair and a long nose. Everything about her is perfect. Her clothes. Her nails. The bright red lipstick on her thin mouth. "Happy?"

"Yes, ma'am."

"Happy?"

"Yes, ma'am."

She shakes her head. "What kind of name is that?" Bug looks at the floor and up again. I see his face, dark with embarrassment.

"The best kind," I say.

Bug grins. "Names are a form of oppression," he says.

"Tate," his mom warns.

Tate? Again, Bug looks away. "People call me Bug," he says.

His mom shakes her head, all disapproval. "Your father called you Bug," she says.

"My name is Bug."

"Fine. Whatever. Can we go?"

Bug sighs. He looks at me. "Yeah," he says.

They walk away. Bug looks back once. He looks miserable. He looks nothing like the Bug I know. His grin's gone. He looks a little frightened. Stressed and out of sorts.

I wait. Fidgety and wired. Wicked thoughts storm around

in my head. Is Mom dead? Did she wreck her car? Maybe someone shot her. Over and over the door opens and people come. An hour passes. Staff comes and tries to make me feel better. He asks if I'm okay. "Maybe she's just late."

"Maybe."

"She'll be here."

"Okay.

"I'm sorry."

"Okay."

Staff takes me to the courtyard. People in shorts and t-shirts and sandals fill the patio. Summer in Portland is precious. Here, rain is a thing. From September to June, everything runs to a gray thickness. When the sun comes north for the summer, Portlanders rush into the warm light, imagining it'll last forever. Small white petals, pale as the summer sky, twist and drift into corners. They speckle the perfect lawn. Helicopter seeds spin in the wind. Starlings and ravens, a robin or two, dance in the sky. They search the grass for food.

Across a small patch of grass, Jules sits with her back to the fence, smoking in the shade of a huge maple. Since she's the only familiar face, I join her. She stares at me with those crazy eyes just long enough to give me a case of the nerves. Today, she's pulled her hair into a tail. Her neck stretches long and white from narrow shoulders.

"Do you want to be alone?" I ask. Jules blinks. "I can... you know. I can sit somewhere else." She taps the ash from her cigarette. "I think I'd...There are just too many people."

Jules's lip twitches. She looks at the patio packed with

visitors. "I hate them," she says. "They come...they have no idea...they just don't know." She grinds her cigarette out in the grass. "This isn't real. None of this. This is all an illusion. They want us to believe we're a community. They want us to believe there's no shame. They take us out of the world, and once a week we get a glimpse... There is nothing dignified about this. They forget about you, don't they?"

I don't know what to do.

"It's okay," Jules says, reaching out a hand, then pulling it back. "They always go away. They go away and we're right here. Always. Me and you."

I don't really understand what she's talking about, but I can't leave either. So, I sit and wait while Jules looks up through the trees at the sky.

"Pretty," she says. She looks at me and for the first time I feel like she actually sees me. She reaches out again, this time taking my hand. "Okay?"

"Yeah."

"Good."

❧

Staff comes with the bell, calling the visitors to the door. People stand. Others lean into their conversations, twisting out the last bit of time as far as they can.

"It's time," Jules says. Her eyes track everyone. People mill. They hug and hang on each other and filter through the door. She looks at me. Her lips are a tight line over her narrow chin. I ask if she's okay and she looks at me. "You and me," she says. "No one comes for us. We're free and pure and we have each other. We keep each other company. You and me. You and me."

She seems to get further away with every word. She seems to fade and it makes me nervous. I want to go. Jules makes me nervous. She isn't like other people. Everything about her is strained. She stands at the edges of things and watches. For the most part, no notices her. She's a speck. A glimmer of light. A passing shadow. But leaving her is hard. I can't just get up and walk away. I can't abandon her here. I owe her something. My time, maybe. My company. It's all I have.

For ten minutes, Staff is busy ushering folks out. Things get loud. Waves of goodbyes. People hugging and kissing. A few tears fall.

Jules holds tight to my hand, her fingers surprisingly strong. "They'll come back," she says. "They always come back. They come and they go, and I'm always here. Waiting. How many times do you think we can do this?"

"Um…"

Jules looks at me and smiles a carnivorous smile. "You were great," she says, lucid for a minute.

"Okay," I mumble. "Thanks."

Jules kisses my cheek and stumbles to her feet. She holds onto my hand for a bit longer, looking down at me. She lets go and wanders away. I watch her go, a bit confused.

When the last of the visitors have disappeared, Staff comes. "Line up, please. Everyone in the hall." One by one and in little groups, we gather. We press our backs to the wall and Staff counts us again. "Okay. Everyone okay?"

Visitation Day sometimes winds people up. Sometimes, things get loud and people need a little extra something. Staff always checks in. They want no trouble so they probe.

We shuffle our feet and look each other. No one says anything. An imperfect silence stretches for just a minute.

"Okay," Staff says. "Dinner in an hour."

I get a smoke from Staff in the Commons and slump in the usual spot on the usual couch.

Curtis comes and walks in tight little circles. He mutters to himself. "Momma says I'm okay. Momma says they're going to let me go. Momma says I'm perfect. Momma says God loves me. I'm a perfect boy. Momma says I'm perfect."

The light through the windows goes all soft and hazy. I stare out at the perfect lawn and the perfect trees. Stringy clouds stretch across a sky gone nearly white. It's beautiful and foreign, as if it belonged to a world I'm no longer a part of. I smoke and I wait and when no one comes, I go to my room. Bug sits on his bed looking a bit drawn.

"Hey," he says.

"You okay?" I ask.

He sighs. His usual goofiness is gone. There's a hardness around his eyes, the corners of his mouth. I wait for him to come back from wherever he's gone. I'm not sure what to say. I watch him and wait and when he looks at me, it scares me. Bug is Bug. Strong. Funny. Beautiful. Right now, though, he seems stretched.

"Can I…is there anything I can do?" Not a real question.

"Sometimes," he says, "I worry. Someday, I'm going to disappear. No one's going to remember me. All I want is for people to remember. I want to do something…I don't want to fade away."

"I'll remember," I say.

Bug shakes his head. I get up. I sit on his bed. Even in this weirdness, he's beautiful. But he's also open now. Vulnerable. I sit next to him and press my thigh against his. He looks at me and smiles, only this smile is sad and worn. Not the usual goofiness or even cockiness. This is something wounded. For the first time, he seems small. He seems frightened. I reach for his hand.

"I promise," I say.

This is it, I think. Slowly, I touch his stubbly chin and his eyes get wide. The kiss is slow and soft. His lips are awfully dry and I'm far too aware of my own face. My tongue feels rough in my mouth. My nose feels too big on my face. But Bug doesn't pull away. He takes the kiss and then he looks me in the eye. He smiles. "Pudge is going to kill me."

"Pudge?"

A grin cuts across his face, a little brittle, not quite back to his ridiculous self. Almost. "We had a bet," he says. "I won."

"A bet?"

Bug wraps an arm around my neck, tight and strong. He kisses me again, gentle and wonderful. "Nothing to worry about," he says.

"Still. A bet?"

"Yeah," he says, kissing my neck, "and I most certainly won."

Pudge is pissed but not really pissed. She slumps on the couch in the Commons. "Unbelievable," she says.

"I told you," Bug says.

"Oh, shut up," Pudge says. "So not fair."

I can't stop thinking of the kiss. It isn't technically my

first. I've kissed men and boys but not because I liked them or because I wanted to. I kissed them to get dope or booze. I kissed them to pass the time. Kissing Bug is real. Fiery and new. It's so out of place. Not that I don't want to kiss him. I like Bug. I like looking at him with his goofiness and sly smiles. Touching him, in the abstract, is thrilling. But then it happened for real and all of the things that come with kissing are suddenly on the table.

Bug presses a hard shoulder into mine. He kisses my cheek. Pudge sighs. Everyone is watching us. Jules comes in. She sits close to the window and stares at me with those intense eyes. At first, it makes me blushy and hot. I can't look at her. Something about the way her face never changes crawls into my belly and turns everything sour. In the end, I look away and when I look back Jules is watching the clouds through the window.

"So sad," Pudge says.

"What?"

"Are you, like, gay?"

"No!" I choke a little. "I mean…I like…girls too…I like…you know."

"I knew it!" she says and presses herself between me and Bug.

"Hey!" Bug says. Pudge kisses my cheek and then Bug's. "Such a hag."

Pudge leans back and giggles. "This is going to be so much fun," she says.

Staff rings the dinner bell. The same bell they ring for everything. Every time I hear the thing, it gets deeper and deeper into my skin. I swallow the irritation and line up with everyone else. Staff comes. He counts us. One by one, he hands us our meals.

Saturdays are burger days and the burgers are hard discs of what might be meat on brittle buns. Bitter pickles and watery tomatoes. The fries are somehow both crisp and soggy. The Jell-O salad is slick and oily.

I sit in my usual place and replay the day. I tell myself that one kiss doesn't make a future. It's just a thing, but I'm not used to things. Not like this. I have this habit of looking for the bad. I can't figure out how or why a kiss changes everything. I can't figure out why it matters.

In Group, they tell us to deal with what's in front of us. Looking forward or back does no one any good. I try to let it go. I try to enjoy the never-ending now, but I can't. I kept thinking *what if* and *why now*. I'm used to being hollow. I'm not used to the buzzing feeling that fills me now, the worry and the want. I'm not sure what to do. So, I decide to do nothing.

Bug and Pudge bring their trays and sandwich me. Again.

"Sweetie," Pudge asks, "why so serious?"

I snap back to reality. Suddenly, I'm in a room with too many people. They watch me and listen for secrets. Panic's edge rises. Queasy. "What?"

"Dude," Bug says, "you look like you kissed a slug."

"No," I say, embarrassed. "I am just thinking… I mean, none of this seems real. I feel… Sometimes, I get the feeling that all this is a figment of my imagination."

"Arrogance!" Bug says.

"No…I mean, I want things and I don't like wanting things. After my dad died…my mom was supposed to be here today. She didn't show…"

"Oh, sweetie," Pudge says, "is that why you're so sad?"

"It's okay," I say. And it is. Kind of. Not really. But what else am I going to say? "After my dad died, I got used to being alone and I got used to not having anyone but then… she says she'll be here and I wait for her and she doesn't even call. I wanted to see her. Mom and I…we don't…we're just people who live… I wanted to see her. I hate it."

Pudge rests a hand on my knee. Bug looks at me with something like worry and sadness.

"She didn't call," I say.

"Doesn't matter," Bug says. "Just a thing." His voice is hard and he won't look at me. "Moms…"

"Right," I say.

We get quiet for a little bit. Thoughts crowd around us, fragments and tatters.

"Sweetie," Pudge says, "it's okay. Really."

"Yeah."

She squeezes my knee. I look at her and I try to feel better but there is no better, just the now and the now sucks. Pudge leans in. Her lips are warm against my ear, her voice is moist and gentle. "If you're a good boy," she says, "I have a present for you."

"A present?"

"Visitation Day," Bug says, all grins and maniacal glee.

I'm not sure what's happening, but it seems promising.

I eat what I can. Not a lot. Three or four bites of burger. Five or six fries. They taste vaguely of dish soap. I don't even try the Jell-O. Everything sits in my gut, a load of stones.

"Dude," Bug says, "you're going to starve."

"I ate."

"Technically."

Pudge squeezes close. "Leave the boy alone."

Bug raises his hands, surrendering. Pudge finishes her plate and takes mine. Watching her eat is fascinating. She obviously hates everything about it but she can't stop. If there's food in front of her, she can't help herself. She looks at me looking at her and goes really still. "What?"

Bug lays a hand on the back of my neck. I turn to him and he shakes his head, just a little, enough to warn me. Pudge glances down at her plate and turns red. She looks at me. She sets the tray down. Too late. It's already empty.

"Pudge…" Bug says. She stands, all rigid lines now. "Pudge, listen…"

Pudge shakes her head. Her face is hard, as if she's keeping something in. She leaves us there. Bug looks bothered. I say I am sorry. He just shakes his head. He reaches out and takes my hand and we wait.

Pudge and Bug are by far my best friends. They're my only friends. Never having had friends, I don't know what to do. I know I've crossed a line, but I don't know what the line is, and I don't know how to uncross it. Having no one around, being unconnected and apathetic, keeps things simple. Things are no longer simple, and I'm not sure how much I like it.

I sit on the couch holding Bug's hand, feeling shitty and small. "It's okay. She has this thing…. You know, food."

"Did I…?"

Bug shakes his head. "She'll be fine."

"Really?" He shrugs. "I'm sorry," I say.

He tries to smile. He tries to make me feel better. "It's okay." He squeezes my hand. We both know it isn't, but there's nothing we can do.

It takes Pudge half an hour to come back. Thirty minutes I spend staring at the doorway, waiting to do something. Anything to make myself feel better. When Pudge comes back, she's pale, sick-looking. Sweaty and shaking. She stops in the doorway. Bug looks up.

"Listen," I say when she slides back down next to me. She holds up a hand and shakes her head. "I wasn't saying anything."

"It's okay," she says.

"No," I say and sigh. Pudge looks at me out of the corner of her eyes. "Really."

"Happy," Bug says, "are you trying to get into her pants?"

Pudge laughs. I don't. "Sweetie," she says, "we're okay." Something in my face catches her eye. "Serious," she says, and takes my hand. "We're okay." She looks at Bug. "You ready?"

The way his face lights up scares me a little. "Let's do it," he says.

I follow them down the hall to an alcove I didn't know was there. Beanbag chairs. A small table bolted to the floor. Dim lights. No windows. Private. Kind of. Private enough.

"Welcome," Pudge says, "to the Meditation Room."

Something's about to happen. Anticipation and surprise are never my thing. I hate waiting for things. I really hate waiting for something and not knowing what I'm waiting for.

"Are you ready?" Pudge asks.

Bug practically quivers with excitement. His eyes are bright in the thin light falling through the door. Pudge, on the other hand, is nearly serene. Nearly divine. All of it—the darkness and the secrecy, the hiding in this little room no one seems to know about—makes me nervous. We settle into the soft seats. Voices drift in the hall. The sound of Staff walking rounds.

"You, my young and quiet friend," Pudge says to me, "you are about to become part of something special."

"Okay."

"What happens here is secret," she says, reaching into her pocket. She brings out a sandwich bag rolled and folded. "Happy Visitation Day.".

"Visitation Day!" Bug says, too loud.

Pudge hushes him and unfolds the bag. Small white pills fill the bottom. Lots of them. I sit. Awkward and hopeful. Pudge beams at me. Bug grabs my leg and shakes me.

"Have you ever done Oxy?" Pudge asks.

My face gets all sweaty. "How…?"

Pudge grins. "Mom," she says.

"Your mom?"

"She feels bad," Pudge says. "You know, because she called the cops when I…when things got bad." She gives us each three pills. "Guilt can be a wonderful thing."

The high comes on slow, a creeping wave of heat and

comfort and bliss. Thoughts unravel. Everything gets soft and distant. Hazy. It's a familiar feeling. I feel just a little sick. That's how real dope works. A little nausea for euphoria.

We sit on the beanbags, holding hands and not talking until Staff comes. "What're you three up to?" he asks. We blink. "I've been looking for you."

"We're right here," Bug says.

Staff tilts his head and stares at us. Suspicious.

A flash of panic. Not real panic. Real panic spins me into a sweat. This panic is far off and feels like something I should feel, instead of something I actually feel.

"We were just…" Pudge says, "you know. Talking."

"We're starting the movie," Staff says.

"Okay," I say.

Staff stands for just a second before leaving. Bug lays his head on my shoulder.

Pudge kisses my cheek. "Popcorn," she says.

"Absolutely," Bug says.

Moving slowly, we go back to the Commons. My nose itches and my fingertips go numb. Again, I find myself stuck between Bug and Pudge, but it doesn't matter. I like the pressure of them sitting tight against me. It's comforting. None of us speak. We watch everything in the same way we watch the hummingbirds in the courtyard. Things are pretty and somewhat interesting but they're abstract and incomplete too. I understand them the way I understand the sunrise or the way rain falls.

Staff hands out cigarettes and large bowls of popcorn, and puts the movie on. *The Breakfast Club.* I've seen it, but not in a while. Because there's nothing else to do, everyone crams into the Commons, even if the room is a bit too small to fit all of us. The couches fill. People stretch out on the floor. Staff allows us to bring blankets and pillows.

Pudge lays her head on my shoulder and Bug holds my hand. The movie plays. A simple story. An "us against them" thing. Kids versus adults. Freedom versus rules. The general assumption is that kids will find common ground given a mutual enemy. Slyly, Pudge slips a hand into my lap, inching closer and closer to my crotch. When she grabs my dick, I jump.

"What?" Bug asks.

"Nothing."

Pudge giggles a little and kisses my neck. I don't know what to do, so I do nothing.

Toward the end of the movie, everyone in the film finally sees each other as real people. They walk away more complete than they were at the beginning. Feel-good bullshit. For the moment, just like in the movie, I'm part of something. No matter how temporary and superficial. I'm part of something and it's nice. We're quiet for a long time. People come and go. Staff gathers the popcorn bowls and rings the damned bell. Everyone lines up in the hall again and Staff counts us. "Lights out in ten."

Everyone goes their own way. Pudge kisses my cheek. "Nighty, night," she says.

"Night," I say.

Bug wraps an arm around my shoulders. His hip thumps mine all the way to our room. I feel bashful and warm. The high from the pills fades but doesn't vanish. Bug undresses and slides into bed. I go to the window and look out at the night. My face hangs in the dark glass, grayish and translucent. All the pieces seem to come apart. Cheekbones disconnect from my jaw. My forehead floats over too-big eyes. My chin's a wedge under my pale lips. None of it's real. None of it makes sense.

"Dude," Bug says, "you okay?" His voice is mushed. The words are slurred and thick.

"Going to take a shower," I say.

"Okay."

I sit on the shower floor. Warm, soft water slithers over me. Steam rises in thin streams and rolls against the ceiling. I run a finger along the grout and a weird joy fills me. Everything falls away. Maybe I sleep. Maybe not. I dream. Maybe not.

Bug comes out of nowhere. He pushes through the curtain. Naked. His glorious chest broad and dark. Mist catches on his stubbly chin. He says nothing, just steps into the shower, his dick hangs hard right in my face.

This is happening, I think.

I kiss first one thigh, then the other. His muscular ass is glorious under my hands. I stand and Bug kisses me. "Hey," he says.

"Hey."

One hand brushes across my belly. The other takes my chin. "You don't have to," he says.

"I know." Something like electricity buzzes in the center of my chest. He runs his fingernails down through my pubic hair and grabs my dick. Fear rattles through me. "Hey," I whisper.

"*Shhhhh.*"

I think of stopping, but I don't want to. We kiss and his lips taste of smoke. I can smell his sweat, sweet somehow and musky at the same time. The roughness of his tongue surprises me, swirling around the inside of my mouth, against my teeth. My hands slide along his back, grab the muscles in his shoulders, his ass.

It's a wild and frantic fuck. Over fast. Too fast. He looks at me. "You know what?" he asks.

"Hmm."

"I can…maybe…someday…fall in love with you."

I don't know what to say. I can't say it back. I can't say anything. He kisses me one more time and leaves. I stand there a long time. Bug's already sleeping when I finally get to bed.

Sleep comes inch by inch. Things drop away. My thoughts settle into long waves. Dreams flicker in fragments. Nothing I can remember. Just enough to leave me tense and sweaty. I wake and my mind races. Details come and go. Bug's lips. His hands. The taste of his sweet skin. Because Staff doesn't let us out of our rooms after lights out, I have nowhere to go. I lie quiet and still and listen to Bug snore.

The hours pass. Slowly, light fills the window. I sit up and wait. I wait, wanting a cigarette. With the Oxy all washed out, I'm back to feeling sick. My hands shake. Bug grunts once. He farts and rolls over. I'm alone again, surrounded by people. Mornings, it seems, are designed for loneliness. It's quiet and a pearly light fills the room, and I think maybe I'm going to die here, by myself, without ever telling Bug that maybe I can love him too.

A hollowness, an empty ache washes through me. Part of me wants to wake him. Part of me wants to touch him again, if for no other reason than to convince myself that all of this is real.

Just as I'm about to do it, Staff starts shouting. I can hear them running in the hall. Everything sounds panicked. Bug opens his eyes and frowns. He sits up. "What the hell?" he says.

We both go to the door. Down the hall, Staff rushes around. They shout things. People run in and out of a room. More and more people come into the hall.

"In your rooms!" Staff shouts. "Doors closed!"

Some of us do as we're told. Most of us not. We stand and watch and Staff's too busy to worry about us.

"That's Curtis's room," Bug says.

"Yeah?"

"Doesn't look good,"

Pudge's room is one down from Curtis's. She sneaks a look as she comes down to us. "I think Curtis is dead," she says, her voice small and thin, her eyes wide and watery. "I think he finally managed to do it."

Bug shakes his head. "Jesus."

"How'd he…?" I stop. I swallow.

Bug takes my hand. "It's okay."

"I wonder," Pudge says. "I mean…shit."

Staff works for a long time. A team brings a cart and a stretcher, but in the end, they give up and stand around, looking as if someone's kicked them in the gut. I kind of feel bad for them.

Bug and Pudge and I stand in the doorway to our room and watch them wheel the body out. They've thrown a sheet over Curtis. Feet, bare and slightly blue, stick out. Bug and I stand in the door to our room, watching as Staff push the gurney down the hall.

Staff comes. She looks at us and down the hall at the closing Door to the World. "Get dressed," she says, her voice strained. "Breakfast in ten." Lines cut deep in the skin around her mouth and eyes. Her fingers tremble and her voice is weak.

"Breakfast?" Pudge asks. "Seriously?"

"Go on," Staff says.

Bug doesn't shower. He dresses slowly, as if the clothes weigh too much. He moves with a heaviness, muttering under his breath. I sit on my bed and watch him. Everything is stretched.

"Are you okay?" I ask.

He looks at me, his eyes filled with tears. It doesn't make sense. Bug wasn't close to Curtis. Curtis was furniture. Part of C-Ward but not part of our lives.

"Hey," I say.

Bug shakes his head. "Someone died today."

"Someone dies every day," I say, more than a little surprised at my own callousness.

Bug looks like I'd slapped him. "How can you say that?"

I swallow. I tell myself I should feel something other than this indifference. I tell myself that I should be ashamed at the cold thoughts flickering through my mind. I worry that maybe I really am less than human. Faced with tragedy, I'm empty as a cracked vase.

"I'm sorry. It's just…I don't know what I'm supposed to feel."

"How about sadness?" Bug asks. "How about horror?"

"Bug…"

"No!" he shouts. "No! Curtis is dead. A boy died. Alone. In the night. There was no one there. There should have been someone there. He died because there was no one there to stop him." A wildness fills Bug's voice. He gets louder and louder. I stand and I try to hug him, but he pushes me away. "He died," he says. "And you act like…"

"I'm sorry," I say.

"Jesus."

"I didn't know him," I say. "None of us did."

"Doesn't matter!" Bug shouted. "Doesn't fucking matter!"

Staff comes and pushes the door open. Bug throws his hands in the air. Tears and snot swing from his chin. Staff grabs Bug's wrists, tight but gentle. "Come on," she says, taking him into the hall. A different Staff turns to me. "You okay?"

"I'm fine."

She nods and closes the door behind her.

Pudge catches up with me in the Commons. I nurse a coffee and a cigarette. She sits next to me on the couch with a sigh. Wet hair clings to her face. She looks pale, stressed. The end of her cigarette trembles.

"Hey," she says. "I heard Bug kind of lost it."

"Yeah."

"What happened?"

I shake my head. We're quiet for a long time.

"This is three kinds of shitty," Pudge says.

"Yeah."

Breakfast is tense. People whisper their conversations. A few folks cry. Quietly. I'm not hungry. For once, Staff isn't watching so I ignore the food. Pudge keeps her head on my shoulder. "Do you think he was scared?" she asks.

"What?"

"Curtis."

"I don't know." A long quiet. "Are you okay?"

Pudge sits up and wipes her nose with a napkin. "I don't know," she says. "It's hard."

"You didn't know him," I say. "No one did."

Pudge shakes her head. "Doesn't matter."

I want to say something. Anything. I want to make her feel better. I want to make myself feel better. Everything's raw and broken, but my feelings aren't my feelings. They come from far away, watery and tired. They feel more like memories of feelings than actual feelings. It's all detached and vague.

Back home, when I got like this, I had pills and I had the straight razor I'd stolen from Dad's shaving kit. I could cut the numbness out. Blood and pain, real, physical pain, focused everything.

But there is no cutting here and there are no pills and there is no darkness to hide in. Here, I have to feel what I feel. I have to feel what I don't feel.

"He's dead," I say.

Maybe if I say it enough, I'll wrap my head around it. I remember the shrouded body. Part of me expects Curtis to come in, talking to himself. And part of me expects this all to be some elaborately cruel joke. No one paid Curtis any attention when he was alive. Dead, he's a hero. He's a warrior fallen in some grand, unknowable war. People take the whole thing entirely too personally. None of them knew anything about Curtis outside of his tendency to make everyone around him uncomfortable.

"He's dead," I say again.

Nothing. Just the guilt of not feeling guilty. And the worry of not feeling much of anything at all.

Pudge puts her head back on my shoulder. "I know," she says.

"Do you think," I begin, then stop. "Do you think he gave up because…do you think…?" Pudge sighs again. "Sorry."

"It's okay."

We sit like that, ignoring everyone, wrapped in the tragedy of having lived when Curtis, who was irritating and weird, didn't.

After breakfast, Staff crowds everyone into the Commons. Bug shuffles in, heavy-eyed and slow. He stops when he sees me. Pudge holds out a hand. "Bug," she says.

He doesn't move. He simply stands in front of us, blinking and swaying a little. Completely stoned. I look at his eyes but only for a minute. There's nothing there I want to see. If he hates me…if he wants nothing more to do with me…

"Sweetie," Pudge says, pulling me close. "Come. Sit."

Bug doesn't move. "Dude," he says.

"It's okay," Pudge says. "Sit."

This time, he takes the step. His knees give out, putting him half in my lap. I wrap my arms around him and slide him into his spot between me and the couch's arm. "Sorry," he says.

"Sweetie," Pudge says, "are you okay?"

Bug looks at his hands and then at me before meeting Pudge's eyes. "Sorry," he says again.

"Me too," I say.

He takes my hand.

Jim, who came in on his day off because Curtis killed himself, comes and looks at us all without looking at any of us. He stands in front of us and crosses his arms on his chest. Lines stand out on his face, especially around the eyes. He looks tired. I kind of feel sorry for him. "Everyone here knows what happened this morning," he says.

People get quiet. They look at him like he can fix it. They wait for instructions. Jim is good at telling people how they should feel. Everyone wants him to tell them that this is all just a thing, nothing to worry about. He doesn't.

"It's a tragedy," Jim says. "One of our own has died."

Our own? I think. Curtis wasn't one of us. He hadn't belonged to anyone. He was a stone in a stream of people. Things moved around him without thought or purpose.

"Curtis is dead," Jim says.

The words fall into a vast silence. Bug flinches. I squeeze his hand. Tears run from his thick eyes.

"There's nothing we can do for him now," Jim says.

"Except…we need to take care of the living. We need to take care of you."

"He was alone," Bug says. "There was no one there…"

Murmurs. Whispers. More tears and sniffling. Jim holds up a hand.

"Everyone will have a chance…" Jim says. "The important thing to remember is that you need to keep yourselves safe. If you start thinking…we will talk to each of you but if you start…if you need anything, anything at all, come to us."

For a long time, no one does anything. No one but Jim. He skims the faces, looking for something. A warning. A weakness. A sign. Whatever it is, he doesn't find it. He bows a little. But then Staff comes and says something. Jim pulls on his shrink face and goes back to work.

"Poor Jim," Pudge says.

"Poor Jim?"

"He looks…" she says. "I don't know. Haunted."

"It's his job," I say. Pudge tilts her head to look me in the eye. "What?"

"Nothing."

"Pudge."

"It's okay."

She sits up. "I need a smoke," she says.

"Pudge," I say, "I'm sorry."

"Yeah?…Okay."

She walks across the room. She looks back at me. Staff gives her a cigarette.

"Pain is pain," Bug says.

"Not if you're dead," I say.

"Nope," Bug says. "Not if you're dead."

❧

We sit. It's Sunday. No Group. We sit. Because Curtis killed himself, Staff watches us. People cry. They hug each other. Rumors float. Staff gives us no details, so we fill the holes with our imaginations. Curtis could have squirreled away enough pills to do the job. He could've found a way to make something sharp enough to cut through skin and muscle and tendon. He might've hanged himself. If he did it right, a bedsheet would've worked or dental floss.

I sit very still between Pudge and Bug and work hard at not thinking about Curtis. But not thinking about something is impossible. Not thinking is a kind of thinking. I drift. Images come and go. Things spin and crash. I'm no good at slowing things down. I'm no good at serenity.

Pudge whimpers and Bug dozes, doped. I breathe and close my eyes. I pretend to fall into an incomprehensible pit. I imagine sitting in a warm vacuum. No thoughts. No feelings. Absolute detachment. I imagine I'm dead, too. I'm everywhere and nowhere. It's a false comfort.

"Sweetie," Pudge says. I shake my head. "Where are you?"

I look up at the ceiling and count the holes in the tiles there.

Back home, when I didn't want to think of something, I got high, and when getting high wasn't enough, I cut. The long scar running along my forearm itches with the memory of steel parting flesh and muscle. Remembered blood warms the palm of my hand. Off and on, something like calm swells for a second or two before the humming anxiety flares and burns it away.

"Sweetie," Pudge says, "it's okay."

"Okay," Bug murmurs, the word thick and slippery.

"It's not," I say.

"No?"

"No." Pudge looks up at me. Her face is pale. "What?" I ask.

"Nothing."

I think about Dad. I hate thinking about Dad. When I do, I think of how cold his hand was and the blood running into the bathtub drain. I try not to think of the clumps splattered on the walls. I remember the way I felt when the paramedics took him away. *I am broken and I don't know how to put the pieces together. I am alone.* My thoughts rattle in my head, cutting at me, leaving me raw

Now that Curtis is dead, Dad comes back to me. Not his face. Too much time has passed for that. Mom has photos but I never look at them. Looking at Dad's face stirred shit up. Not his smell or the memory of his hands. Not his smile or his frown. Not even the sound of his voice. All that faded fast. A month after the funeral, I saw Mom on the couch looking through an album. She made me sit with her and look at the pictures. Dad was already a stranger. A pale man who belonged to a different world. Mom's world.

When I think of Dad now, I think of ragged edges and awkwardness. I think of all the nights I couldn't sleep and the nightmares. Before, when I thought of Dad, I got high.

"Hey," I say.

Pudge looks up. She sits up and looks around. No one looks at us. "I'll help you get Bug to bed," she says. A plan.

A good plan. We stand and drag Bug to his feet. "Come on, sweetie."

We wobble down the hall, Bug between us. "Curtis," he mumbles. "Poor Curtis."

"Yeah," I say.

When we reach Curtis's door, Bug pulls up short. "We didn't know him."

"Sweetie," Pudge says.

"Do you think…maybe he wanted too much?"

"Bug," I say. "Bed time."

"I was thinking," Bug says, "earlier…I was thinking… earlier, you know what Funk said, all about lives and examining and all that bullshit…I am thinking the poor fucker has no idea." He closes his eyes and sways, just a little, like a flower in a rainstorm. He grabs hold of my arm and for the first time since they wheeled Curtis out of C-Ward, there's a flicker of last night's fire, followed immediately by something like guilt. "If you look too close," Bug says. "If you see the wheels and the reasons…life loses its magic. Curtis…he looked too close…poor fucker."

Once we get Bug in bed, Pudge goes to the desk and crushes two pills into powder. She cuts it into rough lines. "There you go," she says.

"Thanks."

She stands in the doorway for a second. "Happy," she says, "don't look too close."

"Okay."

She smiles a thin and brittle smile. "I'm going to take a nap," she says.

"Me too."

I do the lines and I wash my face. I wait for the euphoria to take everything away. My body goes warm and my thoughts get clear. Memories and anger and fear and a weird need to know death's details mix with an opiate calm.

Images play like a knot of mice in my head. I become Curtis but not Curtis. I'm both myself and not myself. I choke but I can breathe. I twitch without moving. A slow wave of darkness and dizziness swells through me. I wait on a dark doorstep to die but it never happens. Panic, remote and thick, mingled with peace and apathy. If I died, I died.

But then I think of Jim calling Mom. Her face twists and break. I've seen that once before, when Mom found me holding Dad's hand in the bathroom. I was eleven and everything meaningful dropped out of her. We both became slightly less human. It took only an instant. Death became a reality. I learned to live like I was already dead. Remote. Empty.

The window in our room opens just four inches. The air coming through is warm and smells of lilacs. Tiny ants march along the sill in a ragged line. One by one, I crush them with my thumb. Their shells crunch. Death is sudden and unforgiving. I'm a god, if only to ants. If only when I'm alone.

Ants die and Bug snores. He rolls onto his belly. One magnificent shoulder strains against his shirt. A long muscle stretches from his jaw down to his collarbone. I reach out. Not thinking. My hand is someone else's. My finger traces the line of his jaw. He bats at me.

"Are you okay?" I ask. Nothing. "Bug, are you in there?"

More nothing. "Are you going away?"

The door swings open. Staff looks in. She looks nervous for a moment, but then she sees me and her face changes. A gentle hardness in her jaw. She smiles without smiling. A very nurse-like habit. "Happy," she says. I look up. "Jim wants to talk to you." I don't move. "Happy?"

"Yeah."

"Are you okay?" Somehow my hand finds its way back to my lap. Staff straightens. She frowns. "Happy?"

"Yeah."

Narrowed eyes look for something. They shift from me to Bug to me again. "What…?" She stops. She swallows. "Happy," she says. "Jim…"

"Okay."

"Now."

"Okay."

Pretending I'm not high is hard. My nose runs and my lips burn. I have no practice. Back home, no one cared. No one noticed. But here, in Jim's bland little office with its simple table and simple chairs and the walls rising over us, empty and smooth, hiding is impossible.

Jim stares at me warily. "Are you okay?" he asks.

"What?"

"Happy…"

"I'm fine."

The skin around Jim's eyes gets tight. His lips thin. "You look…you seem…out of it," he says.

"Sorry."

Jim sighs. Lines get deep between his eyebrows. He looks

worn and worried. He looks like he's trying to do too much. Maybe Pudge is right. Maybe Jim is poor Jim. Maybe he is haunted. I don't want to think about that. "Have you eaten?"

"Shocks the system."

"Happy," Jim says. "You have to take care—"

"I'm just…you know. Dead boy and everything."

Jim waits. It's a therapy trick. He sits. Silent. I decide to wait him out. He's better at it than I. He sits and I sit. The air gets thick. I give up.

"Do you ever get the feeling…?" I begin. The thought runs out. Confusion rolls over me. Everything goes kind of dim. Words dribble away into fractured thoughts. Things spin a little. The Oxy calm is slipping away. All I have left is the memory of a comfort that isn't all that comfortable. Still, I try to hold onto it. A greasy panic spreads out from my gut to the tips of my fingers and toes. "I watched them take him out."

Jim leans forward. A weird light illuminates his face. Nothing physical. He's still bland to the point of near invisibility. But he's suddenly sharper, as if the words I might say are the answer to some world-changing riddle.

"I watched them take him out," I say. "Curtis. I saw the body…and none of it…it isn't real."

Something stands between us. It keeps us from understanding each other. Nothing gets through. Not completely.

"Happy," Jim says, "it's very real."

I wave my hands at him. "I can't believe… Just yesterday, I saw…Curtis is here. Doing his thing. You know? He is talking and I see him…he is part of my world."

"It's okay," Jim says.

"You're not listening!" The words were far sharper than I had intended. Jim leans away from me, defensive. "It's not real. Like when my dad…people come and go. They are the walls around us. You know?" My fingertips rasp against each other. "I can't imagine… Curtis won't be there when…if I walk out of this room…will he be there? Will he be there… doing his circles and…and…doing what he always does."

"Death is hard," Jim says.

"It's impossible."

"It's inevitable," Jim says. "Nothing to be afraid of."

"I'm not afraid."

"Happy, it's okay."

"Things," I say. "Two things…either he is here and is still here…you know…out there, waiting. Or…or…he was never here, and I'm just now figuring it out."

"Happy," Jim says. I make a fist. Jim's face goes rigid and still. "I need you to calm down."

I suck air into my lungs and close my eyes. "I'm fine."

Jim isn't convinced. He looks like he's ready to run.

"Do you ever get the feeling that you're the only one?" I ask. Jim blinks. I wait and he waits longer. "Never mind."

"No."

"It's just…just…sometimes I get the feeling that I'm the only one here."

Jim is really paying attention now. Wide-eyed and thin-lipped. He makes notes without looking at the pad in front of him. For a moment, that distracts me. Part of me wants to know how he can write without looking at what he's writing. "What're you saying?" Jim asks.

Words boil. None them the right words. "Listen," I say. "I… I'm the only one. That's what I'm saying. There's no one else here."

"I'm here."

"What if you're not real? What if this...this shit we call reality, what if it's not real?"

"Happy," he says. "It's real."

"Maybe."

Jim laces his fingers under his nose. I watch the thoughts playing in his eyes. Something comes to him. Something hard. Something very shrinkish. "What're you worried about?" he asks, a little harshly. "Everything's right here."

"What if it's fake?"

"Just touch it," he says.

Touch it? I stretch one hand out. I touch the table. Not cold. Not warm. Hard and smooth. "I worry…Never mind."

"No," Jim says, with a sigh. He puts his pen on the table. I think for a moment he's going to grab me. "Who're you talking about?"

"What if I'm the only one?"

"The only one what?"

Something inside comes loose. Something breaks and the words pour out. I kick myself to my feet. Jim scrambles back. Pale. Shaking. "The only one in the world!" I shout. "Maybe in the whole universe. I don't know. Maybe it's all a dream."

"It's not a dream," he says, quietly.

The words quiver but stand.

"But it can be, you know? Maybe out there, where everything's real…"

"Everything's real here."

Everything in him tries to convince me. Fear ruins his habitual blandness. Part of me feels sorry for him. I want to stop, but I can't. It goes on and on. Waves of heat and tingling cold ripple along my spine. "You don't know that."

"I do," he says. "I promise. I know."

I go still. Quiet. "What's out there, then?"

"Everything," he says. "The world."

"Prove it."

A question forms on his lips. He reaches out a hand, slowly. We stand like that for a moment. After a bit, I take it. Jim blinks. I nod. He nods.

We stand. We go out to the hall. To a window. A beetle of some sort scuttles on a leaf. Grass stretches in a perfect swatch from here to the hedges at the edge of the lawn.

"See," he says.

I see everything. "Okay." We turn our backs. I stop. Jim frowns. "Is it still there?"

"Dear God."

"It might've gone away."

"It hasn't."

"Okay"

We start back to the office. People watch us. Pudge stands in the Commons door. She makes a face.

"It doesn't matter," I say. "Things don't go away when you watch them. They wait for you to turn your back."

Jim shakes his head. "There can be this thing…"

"Is it real?" I ask.

Jim's smile falters when I looked at him. "I don't know! It's just this huge thing sleeping, dreaming all this…this shit we call reality."

"But is it real?" I ask again.

Jim opens the door. I wait for him to sit. He waits for me. "It doesn't matter," he says with a flash of agitation. "If it's not real, nothing can happen."

"Yes, it can," I say. "Shit happens all the time. Doesn't matter if it's real or not. If people think it's real..."

"But if it's not—"

"It can all end right now," I say. "It can all just stop and no one'd know it, because we'd all be gone."

Jim palms his face. I'm getting to him, and I kind of feel bad about it. Worry and frustration etch themselves around his mouth and eyes.

"What if it's my dream?" I ask.

"Happy...this isn't...I'm worried about you."

"This could be a figment of my imagination, Jim. You ever think of that? If I'm making all this up, then that makes me God, doesn't it?"

"Not funny."

"I'm not trying to be funny. I don't want to be God. They killed the last guy who said he was God. I don't want to be killed. Especially by people who might not even exist."

Jim makes more notes. "No one's trying to kill you."

"I can be God."

Jim writes frantically. "Delusions of grandeur..."

"I think you're just pissed."

"Not pissed."

"You don't get to be real," I say.

Jim looks up at me. "Not funny."

"No," I say, "not funny at all."

"Go on," Jim says. "I think we're done."

He stops looking at me. He writes notes. I want to know what he's writing but I don't want to ask. Part of me wants to go. I can't. I stand.

"Jim" He looks up. "I'm sorry."

"Yeah?"

"I'm trying."

He tilts his head one way, then the other. Curious. Like a dog trying to decide if he wants to bite me or not. "I don't think you are," he says. Harsh. "Blasphemy. Mockery."

"I didn't mean to hurt your feelings."

A frown. He sets his pen on the table. "We're done."

A nastiness comes to mind. I open my mouth and close it. "Okay."

I slip into the Commons.

"Are you okay?" Staff asks.

I look at her.

"You look sad," she says.

"You know," I say, "dead boy."

"Happy…" The disapproval, the judgement stings. "Sorry." She frowns and hands me a cigarette.

A long silence. Not a perfect silence. People walk and talk. Death is a thing to us. We think about it. We flirt with it. We play with it. Every one of us sports scars and carry stories. But few of us know anything about death. Not first hand. We all find a reason not to finish the deed. We find reasons to stop. Not Curtis. Somehow, the animal instinct to survive faded enough to give him room to die.

And now, here it is. Death. Real death. Tragic and

inexplicable death. It tears through us. It leaves us tattered and sore. None of us know what to do. So, we wander and cry and try to make sense of it. It wounds us. Staff and patients both. We do the best we can, but our best is completely insufficient.

I sit in my spot, smoking and watching and remembering. I think about my dad and the way his body lay in the tub. The gun was small and silver and it didn't look real but it was. His brain, splattered on the wall, reminded me of oatmeal. Overcooked. And the smell. Charred meat. Blood's metallic reek. Shit. I remember moving like something vast and invisible controlled me. I was a marionette. Nearly real but not quite.

Things get strange. Dream-like. My body melts into the couch. I hang at the ceiling and watch. Clear-headed. Calm. An almost opiate feeling without the itching and odd skin crawling feelings. Sounds go tinny. Things thin to kind of a shroud. On the far side, something vast, incomprehensible. Giant gnarled joints move. Part of a face. A massive finger pushes through, probing. I am both terrified and thrilled.

But then someone says my name and I slam back into the world. Hard. I jump. My back cracks. "Ow."

Everything in me feels jarred. Bruised. Like I've fallen. My cigarette has though. It burns a small oval hole in the couch. One among many. Still, I feel bad. I crush the cigarette in the ashtray and pick at the burn's charred edges like I can make it go away.

Jules stands over me with her mismatched eyes. Sharper than usual. Like she's more there than before. I look around.

The Commons is neither packed nor empty. When I look back to Jules, she hasn't moved.

"You're here," I say.

"Doesn't count," she says, and settles in next to me. Too close. Everything about her moves. Her fingers pick at invisible specks on her black skirt. A flimsy thing. Thin and flighty. Her heels tap and her knees bounce. She leans across me and taps the ash from her cigarette. Her face gets hawkish. Hair the color of dried blood hangs in long tangles around her pointed face.

"I died once," she says, indifferent, twisting on the couch. "I had it all planned."

"Jules…"

One hand rises and hangs in the air for a second before falling to her lap again. She looks at me with eyes, wide and round and watery. "I had it all figured out," she says.

She pulls her skirt up, almost too high. Inside her thighs, scars ran like a ladder, perfectly measured. One-inch long. Half-inch apart. Vaguely blue. Wrinkled. "My dad…"

I go cold. My back hurts. My ribs and fingers.

"He's dead now," Jules says. "Died in prison." One finger stretches out. It almost touched my shoulder before folding again. "He's dead and still… Sometimes, I think he's still here."

A frown knots the skin around her eyes. The corners of her mouth dig deep in her cheeks.

"My dad," I say, "he died."

Jules leans in. Close. She smells of soap. Her head tilts to the side. "Do you want to kiss me?" she asks.

"Um…"

Jules grins, fleeting and sharp. I cringe. "Never mind," she says. Voices rise and fill the room. I flinch, and Jules goes a little white. "You kissed that boy," she says. "Right?"

I don't know what to say.

"My dad never kissed me," Jules says. "He didn't like kissing… I've never kissed a boy. I've never kissed anyone."

"Sorry."

One shoulder rises. Something goes out of her. She flops back on the couch. Nearly boneless. "I had it all figured out," she says to the ceiling. "I had it planned. I was dead…after they killed…after my dad died…I was dead. I took, like, a hundred Oxies and passed out on this…I went out to this logging road in the middle of nowhere, you know. I was dead, but someone found me and they called the ambulance...I was dead but now…not so much."

Jules touches my forearm, a casual touch. Fingertips run along the scars there. Thicker and more random. Less precise. "You're a good boy," she says.

"I don't know."

Another smile. Gentler. "We're all dead here," Jules says. "Dead and waiting."

I watch her walk away. Anxious. Scared. Not at all sure what just happened.

Staff calls lunch. They ring the damned bell and we all line up. Slowly. Because it's Sunday it takes a bit for people to come from every corner of every room. Many are raw-faced and torn up over Curtis. A suicide in a locked and secure ward. I guess there's a difference between "locked" and "secure." Pudge comes and cuts the line to stand with me. She grabs my hand and puts her head on my shoulder. Everything about her is quiet. Her hair hangs flat, smashed during her nap.

"Sweetie," she says. I kiss her forehead. It tastes of shampoo and cigarette smoke. Bug comes. Sluggish. "Nice nap?" Pudge asks.

Bug tilts his head. "Not bad," he says, "but then I had help."

"All right, folks," Staff says, "settle."

We press our backs to the wall and wait. Staff counts us. They let us eat outside. We take lawn chairs to the shade along the fence. Nature's apathy is stunning. A boy is dead and the grass grows. The wind blows. Helicopter seeds whirl in the sunshine. Ravens play in the sky. It isn't a calculated indifference. It's more inherent. Nature, the world, can't be bothered to notice a single death. Everything's a machine, and the machine rumbles on with or without us. Everything is bright and more than a little hot. Butterflies flutter from flower to flower. Bees bounce around the rhodies.

A weird sense of something. Questions. I feel out of order and removed. A strange numbness inside and out. Things happen around me. Not *to* me. I live in an amber light. A life half dead. Empty, and oddly both full and empty.

Lunch is spaghetti and meatballs. I'm not hungry. I poke at the limp noodles and the gray broccoli. Pudge attacks her food as if she has to kill it before eating. Stabbing. Scooping. Chewing. I roll meatballs around my plate and toss them one by one into the brambles. I stir the noodles up enough to make it look like I ate something. I set the fork on the tray.

"Sweetie," Pudge says, "what's wrong?"

"Do you think we ever…do you think we'll ever get out?" I ask. Pudge frowns. "I've been thinking…I've been wondering if we'll ever get out. I've been here, like, weeks and I forget…Curtis is dead. I forget what it's like. Being here, in this place, with these walls…nothing's real…after my dad…I am numb."

"Sweetie," Pudge says, "it's okay."

I shake my head. "It's not. I can't stop…things come and go and I…I hate this."

"We all do," Bug says.

"I just think about getting out of here and then what? I mean, shit…people die…people go away…they leave. Sometimes, for just a while. Sometimes forever."

"Sweetie," Pudge says, "I'm right here."

"But how long?"

"Dude," Bug says.

I talk over him. "People are dying. They die and we have to stay here and think about them. My dad…I can't remember him. Not really. I remember this blurry feeling, no details. Just…I can't…my dad died and I forgot about him, and now, Curtis. I loved my dad. I didn't know Curtis. He was just this guy and now he's dead and he's gone, and I can't remember my dad and I think about Curtis…he's already gone."

I look up at the sky, the unsympathetic sky.

"Did you know that for most of history…for most of human existence…a hundred years ago, I'd have been on my own, all grown up, having kids. I'd have been working. No planning. No time to think about the future because, you know, I'd have been too busy living...But now, I have all this time to think, to remember."

"Sweetie," Pudge says, "it's okay."

I look her in the eye. I look from her to Bug. "If we get out of here, you have to promise...you have to remember."

Bug takes one hand and Pudge the other. "Dude," Bug says.

"No one's going to forget you," Pudge says.

"Guys..."

"Shut up," Bug says and kisses one cheek, Pudge the other. My face remembers their lips for a long time.

"Guys..."

"Hush," Pudge says.

After lunch, Staff does the bell thing. They do the counting thing. And they crowd us into the Commons again. Too many bodies in too small a room. Too many voices talking about too many things. Some grumbling because it's Sunday and there's supposed to be no Group. Jim holds up a hand. Most of us shut up.

"There are rumors going around," he says, his voice all gravel and glass. "There are stories being told. It needs to stop. What happened today was a tragedy. But you're young... you can't use this..." A sigh. Whispers. Jim looks at the ceiling and then out the window before continuing, his voice hard—everything about him, brittle—"There is nothing romantic or gallant about what happened. It's heartbreaking. Don't make things harder than they need to be."

He goes on but I stop paying attention. I'm tired. I'm sad and confused. I want to close my eyes. I'm done.

"Sweetie," Pudge says.

"He talks too much," I say.

She smiles. "He has all the answers," she says.

"Sure," Bug says. "Just ask him."

Staff dismisses us to C-Ward's various corners for the day. They pass out cigarettes. Pudge hooks a leg over mine. Bug pretends that his hip pressing against mine has nothing to do with him.

Things are getting back to normal. Fast. People talk and Staff watches and the day passes. It amazes me a little how the passing hours can take something like a boy's suicide and make it dull and routine. Already, Curtis's face fades. I remember, in the abstract, him wandering in circles, muttering and praying. I remember the awkwardness I felt whenever he was in the room.

"Do you think they'll let us have a wake?" Pudge asks.

"Never happen," Bug says.

"Why not?"

"A wake?" Bug raises his eyebrows. "Come on."

"Stupid," Pudge says.

The thing about other people's pain is that it's always washed-out when mixed with our own.

"Sweetie," Pudge says.

"He's already just a story," I say.

"What?" Bug asks.

"Curtis. He's one of those stories we'll tell over beers someday."

"God," Bug says. "Beer."

"He's not even a memory," I say.

"It's okay," Pudge says, putting her head on my shoulder.

Bug stretches and drapes an arm around my shoulders.

"Dude," he says, "we all need stories."

I look at him and can't stop because Bug is one of those people I want to look at forever. Pudge laces her figures with mine. Her lips are so close to my ear, I can hear her smile. "It's going to be okay," she says.

"Helluva day," Bug says.

"Sweetie," Pudge says. "You didn't know him."

"I know," I say. "Still."

It's a school night. At nine, Staff calls lights out. Pudge kisses my cheek and leaves. Bug and I shuffle silently to our room. I sit on my bed and watch him undress. Watching Bug get naked is a thrill. Broad muscles ripple. I want to touch each line, each scar. I want him to tell me the story behind each one.

He gets naked with a stripper's grace. He knows that I am watching and he likes it. He moves slowly, giving me an eyeful. For just a second, he stands completely naked. He spins, as if looking for something, but we both know it's part of the show. He looks up at me and grins his slightly manic grin.

He looks at the door for a moment before coming to kiss me. His lips are dry and soft. His hand, gentle. I reach out and cup him. Both of us hard and throbbing.

"You're so pretty," he says.

"No."

"Hush," he says. His body is all hard lines and broad planes. He kisses me so hard, I have trouble breathing. We sway. "Bathroom," he says.

We close the door behind us. Bug turns on the shower. We

fuck slowly and completely and quickly.

"Nice," Bug says when it's over.

I kiss him again.

"Boys!" Staff calls.

Bug jumps in the shower. I open the door.

"Yeah?" I say.

"What's going on?"

"Going to the bathroom."

"Where's Bug?"

"Shower."

"Shower?"

"I had to go," I say. "Bad. Bug said it was okay."

Staff's face pinches a little. "One at a time," she says.

"Okay," I say and cross to my bed. "Sorry."

Sleep comes and goes. A dangerous tide. Shallow and fast. Dream riddled. Faceless people. People I know. Strangers, too. The living and the dead. They move and swirl and dance. They pinch away bits of flesh. They pound me with stony hands. I have to save them or kill them. All night, I jump in and out of sleep. In the end, I give up and get up. The night seems old. Morning seems close but I can't be sure.

There are no clocks in C-Ward. Time is both fluid and infinite. I lie for a long time and listen to Bug snore. Staff does Checks, opening the door and closing it. I go to the bathroom. The light startles me. Hurts my eyes.

I piss and shower. Hot water but not hot enough. Water falling but not falling hard enough. None of it helps. None of it matters. I grab a book from my desk.

"Happy," Staff says. "You need to go to bed."

"What?"

"Sleep."

"Can't," I say.

"Happy."

"Nightmares."

"Are you okay?"

It doesn't matter. Insomnia is familiar. "I'm the dead man," I say.

Staff looks confused.

I hold up the book. "Poem."

"You need to rest."

I shake my head.

"Happy," Staff says, "come on."

I set the book on the desk. Staff walks me to the nurses' station. They give me something. A small white pill.

"Go to bed," Staff says. "Sleep. It'll be okay."

"Okay."

"Happy," Staff says.

"I know."

Part Three

Jim calls a meeting. Everyone's going to be there. Jim and Mom and whoever else with a say in my life. Too many people.

"Don't worry about it," Jim says, because, of course, I am worried. "This is just us talking about the progress you've made and what the next step is going to be." He smiles suddenly. "Like a PTA meeting."

"I've never been to a PTA," I say.

Jim blinks and sits back in his chair. "Really?"

"Mom and Dad worked, then Dad died. There were more important things…school wasn't really on the radar."

Jim looks at me for a while, thinking, maybe of something to say. He writes something on his pad. Something fluttery happens in my head.

"What're you writing?" I ask.

Jim frowns. "Notes."

"Can I see them?"

He shakes his head and pulls the pad closer to his chest. "That wouldn't be appropriate.".

"Whatever."

The night before the meeting, Staff catches Bug and me fucking in the shower. It's stupid. Both Bug and I are Level Three and that means we have thirty minutes between Checks. Staff must have heard something because they crash through the bathroom door like a cop storming a crack house. The door slams into the wall. *Bam!* It bounces hard enough to knock Staff off balance for a second. It gives us time for Bug to pull out and cover himself. For some reason, having Staff glaring at me like that does nothing but make me mouthy.

"Hey!" I shout. "What the fuck?"

"Get dressed," Staff snaps, red-faced, standing there in a classic hands-on-hips mother-pose.

"Jesus."

"Now!"

I step out. The floor's cold. "A little privacy," I say.

Staff turns narrow eyes on me. "Mouth," she says. She doesn't move. Neither do I.

Bug pulls the shower curtain over his hips. "We'll be out in a second," he says.

His tone and the look on his face convinces her to leave. First, she looks from me to him and back again. "Two minutes," she says.

"Whatever."

Staff raises a hand, finger pointed but then she shakes her head and leaves.

Bug grabs a towel. "We're so busted," he says. It doesn't matter to me. I'm all wrapped up in the unfairness of it all. "They're totally going to take levels," Bug says. His voice trembles. He sounds truly scared.

"What're they going to do?" I ask. "Lock us in our room?"

"Dude."

I just shake my head and grab a towel. Slowly, Bug and I dress. Bug wears nothing but scrubs pants. His glorious chest and shoulders stand out, shiny still from the shower. I slip into a pair of boxers. Together, we go out to the room.

Staff waits there for us. She stands with a twisted face. Judgmental and stern.

"Listen," I begin.

Staff holds up a hand. "Not now," she says.

"When?" I snap.

Knots form in her forehead. "You might want to mind your tone," she says.

I shake my head and sit on the end of my bed. Bug stands by the window, all red-faced and shy.

"What the…?" Staff says. "You two know the rules."

"Stupid," I say. Staff points a finger at me. "What?" I demand. "What're you going to do?"

"Happy," Staff says, shaking her head, "just get dressed."

"What?"

"You're sleeping in the Quiet Room."

"What? No."

Other Staff come and stand in the doorway. I think about fighting. About pitching a fit but Staff looks ready for it. Bug not so much.

"Happy," Staff says. "Now."

"What the hell for?"

Staff sucks in a big breath. She looks pained. "Now."

From across the room, Bug's voice floated, quiet and quivering. "Dude…Please."

"Bug…"

He won't look at me. "I'll see you in the morning," he says.

"Fine." I grab my jeans and a shirt. "In the morning."

"This way," Staff says.

The Quiet Room is a little room off the nurses' station. Thick padding hangs on the walls, dimpled with heavy buttons. Canvas-covered. Once white. Stained now with blood or shit or vomit. It's impossible to tell. A solid-looking bed stands in the middle of the room, bolted to the hard floor. A plastic mattress lies on the bed frame, cracked and slightly blue. The door's massive. No windows. An industrial lock.

"Really?"

"We'll talk in the morning," Staff says.

"More than likely."

"I'll get a blanket."

"And a pillow."

Staff shakes her head. "No pillow."

"What?"

"Policy."

She shuts the door. Thud. Final. Eternal. The lock sliding home with a sinister snick. Shock. It hits me. This is real. I sit on the bed and try to swallow my breath. I can't feel my fingertips.

"You're okay," I say. "You're fine."

But I'm not. I'm not fine and I'm not buying the lie.

"Fuck. Fuck. Fuck."

Time gets fat and slow. Greasy. I lie on the bed. The hard mattress crackles. A restlessness invades me. I want to move but there's nowhere to go. A small cramp forms in the arch of one foot. I ignore it and close my eyes. I breathe slow, deep breaths.

After a long time, Staff brings a thin blanket. Green.

Wool. Military-looking. Even before I touch it, I can see it's going to itch. She holds it out. I get to my feet. Staff watches me with cautious eyes.

Behind her, another Staff stands with two small paper cups. Pills. Nastiness rises in me, but I keep it in. Things are bad enough. I don't want them to know I care, but maybe they know already. Still, I keep my face hard and flat.

"This'll help you sleep," Staff says.

I take the pill.

"We'll talk in the morning," Staff says.

"This is stupid."

"Policy."

"Policy sucks."

I wrap the bristling blanket around my shoulders and sit on the bed. Staff goes away. The door thumps again. The lock snicks home. I'm alone.

Seclusion. Silence. The sound of my own breathing. Somehow, since coming to C-Ward, I've gotten used to the sound of people. They walk. They talk. There's always something making noise somewhere. The Quiet Room is too quiet. Too empty. After a bit, I pace. I listen to the sound of my bare feet on the hard floor. It's a small, slithering sound. But it's a sound. The view never changes. I try to count the buttons holding the padding to the wall but keep losing track. I try to make images out of the stains, but they flow and change every time I blink.

A camera hangs under a black plastic dome in the corner. I watch it, wondering if people watch me on the other end. I doze on the bed, the kind of half sleep that lends itself to dreams and visions. My mind makes monsters from memories. A snapshot of getting caught stealing candy when I was a kid, flips into a scene of me watching my mother in the shower, which slides into a tableau of holding Dad's hand in the bathroom, blood everywhere.

Anxiety washes through me. It's like someone put a broken television in my head and I can't find a channel. All I can get is static, fuzzy sentences, parts of scenes, shattered faces. White noise fills me up until I can't think, or speak, or even move after a while. My legs twitch, cramp. My shoulders shiver. A sudden need to be somewhere, anywhere else, doing something, presses down on me. My guts knot in an electric burn. Violence bunches up in my arms and head.

Finally, I sleep. Kind of. My neck hurts. I need to piss but not bad, so I ignore it. Time passes in fits and starts. The night lasts forever but then it's over. Faster than I think possible.

Morning comes and Staff opens the door. A tall man. Too thin. Scarecrow-looking. Relief stutters in my gut. I stand.

"Morning," he says. "There's breakfast."

I grunt and shake my head.

"You need to eat," he says.

"Not hungry."

"Not an option."

Staff walks me through empty halls. I follow him but something's off. C-Ward's too calm. Too quiet. We get to the Commons. The breakfast table stands alone in the corner. Things have the stretched feeling of early morning, but the sunlight in the windows is older than that. Nothing feels right.

"Go on," Staff says.

"Where's…?"

"School."

"Can I have a cigarette?"

"Eat," Staff says. "Shower. Your meeting's soon."

He leaves. I stand for a moment. Unsure. A little confused. For a moment, I wonder if this is real. Moving slowly, I drink a bit of orange juice. I eat a few bites of egg. A piece of toast. Bacon. But then I give up and go to my room.

It's the same room but it's different too. I can't put a name to it, but things are off. My bed's the same bed. Blankets bundled at the foot. Sheets twisted into knots. Bug's bed's neat and made. All of his things stand in perfect piles. The air is thick and gray. I shake myself and go to the bathroom.

For some reason, the bathroom is always cold. Getting naked for my shower's a bit of a misery and the shower's never hot enough, but I let the water slither over me for a long time anyway. The white noise is a comfort. It distracts me. Calms me. It's familiar somehow. Peaceful.

I wash myself and when I feel like I should be done, I dry myself and dress in the empty room. I sit on the edge of my bed and wait. I have no idea what's coming. The worry of the coming meeting rushes through me in waves. My feet tap an impatient tempo on the floor. My thighs rub against the denim of my jeans. An old feeling comes back to me. The feeling that none of this is real. Everything's dream-like and strained. I'm both in my body and out of it. Things twist and bend. Color blooms and fades. Sounds echo and vanish.

Finally, Staff comes and takes me down the hall.

"What's happening?"

Staff looks at me strangely. "It's time."

Questions bubble and turn in my head but I put them away and follow Staff to a conference room down by the nurses' station. Part of me expects a courtroom with a judge's bench and witness stands, jury boxes and tables for the lawyers. Instead, I get a room with thin blue carpet and non-challenging pastel abstracts on the walls.

People gather around a long, wooden conference table. There are no lawyers, no judges. Only Jim and a few Staff. And Mom. Everyone watches while I take my place at the table. Mom sits across from me. She looks at me for a moment then she looks at the table. A man sits with her. I don't know him. No one bothers to introduce him. Everything about him is squarish. Square hands and a square head topped with bristly black hair. I don't like him.

"Happy," Jim says. "Let's get this started." He uses his therapist voice. Attentive without paying attention. Every word comes out all caring and reasonable, like he's here only to help. His face is so mild it's impossible to watch for long. It's almost like he isn't really here. I want to throw something at him just to see what he'd do.

Everyone sits up a little straighter and a little more still.

"We all know why we're here," Jim says.

The guy with Mom starts talking about how I was brought in, because of my drinking and getting high, and about how I had told Bruce about wanting to die sometimes. Indifferent and confident, he never once looks at me, but reads from notes on a big, yellow pad. "And now," he says, "even while here, Happy's shown a careless recklessness. Just last night, he was found in questionable activity with another boy. Obviously, Happy's judgement is compromised. We're concerned about his health and fitness. We're very concerned about his safety."

Everyone listens and people write some stuff down. Mom watches me, looking like she wants to cry. She says nothing though. I'm angry now. These people have no idea what my life's like. They have no clue what goes on in my head. I want to walk out. I want to yell. I just shake my head.

Jim makes notes. When he looks up, he looks right at Mom, as if he's trying to figure something out. But then he smiles his non-smile. He starts talking about safety and responsibility. He talks about me. Not to me. He calls Mom, "Mrs. O'Neill." He says her name a lot. A therapy trick designed to make her think he cares. Respects her. He talks about more permanent solutions and taking everyone's well-being very seriously. He leaves out details or plans. He talks in general. Mom nods along, as if she likes what she's hearing.

Jim tells Mom I'm doing well in school. Except for math. He says Funk thinks I have a gift for language. I think of the poems I've been writing. Only Bug and Pudge read them. They're new and raw and private. If Funk sees them, he'll have to report them. All suicide and sadness and sex. If Funk reports them, Jim will know things he has no business knowing. I keep them in the bottom of a drawer in my room.

Jim tells Mom I struggle in Group. He says I seem to have trouble relating to people. Jim tells Mom I have friends, a few anyway, but that I don't seem interested in therapy. He says I'm belligerent at times and indifferent. He doesn't talk about the state of my soul. He talks and people listen. They make notes. I sit and wait. No one looks at me.

A fly buzzes up near the lights. Bumping and bumbling around. A space around the light is a different color than the rest of the room.

"Happy," Jim says, "do you understand the question?"

"What?" I blink.

Mom looks at her hands. Her nails bleed a little. She picks at herself when she's stressed. A habit she started after Dad died. Jim stares at me. Wrinkles branch out across his temples and the tops of his cheeks. "Do you understand what's happening?" he asks again.

"It's stupid," I say.

"What is?"

"All of it."

Jim smiles and writes something. The man next to Mom makes a note too. It pisses me off. People are always writing stuff about me.

"You want to tell me what's stupid?" the man asks.

"Who are you?"

He frowns at me. "I'm your mother's lawyer."

"Lawyer?"

"I'm here to make sure everyone's rights are respected."

"Okay."

"Can you tell me what's stupid?" he asks again.

I have to think about it for a second. There are no answers, but I have to say something. "I don't know," I say.

"Do you really want to die?" he asks.

"Sometimes."

"Why?"

"I don't know. Sometimes it's just not worth it."

"What's not worth it?"

Everyone watches me. I look around, but no one looks away. They aren't scared. They know what they're doing here, so I just watch my fingertips against the wood of the table. White crescent moons grow along the edge of my nails. I peel them off one by one and flip the torn pieces over my shoulder. I look up.

"All of it." I tap my fingertips against the tabletop. "I just don't get it. What's it matter to you if I kill myself?"

"Because it matters," he says—as if he means it.

"Whatever."

Something washes through the lawyer's face for a second, but then he looks down at his pad and writes more notes. "Okay."

"Are we in agreement?" Jim asks.

Agreement? I don't agree to anything. But Mom and her lawyer nod. Jim, too. People gather their papers. They stand. I watch them.

"Happy," Jim asks. "Would you like to spend a little time with your mother?"

I don't know what's happening.

"Happy?" Mom says.

I nod. I shrug. Jim looks at Mom. He holds out a hand. "Mrs. O'Neill," he says.

"Thank you."

Something's off. A blackness swells around Mom's eyes. Her lips are thin and white. Deep creases run in crooked lines through her forehead. "Are you okay?" she asks, reaching across the table. She stops, putting her hand back in her lap. "I miss you."

"Really?"

"Come on," she says, her voice all sad and thick.

"It's been a month."

"I have…it's hard."

"Tell me about it."

"Is it horrible?" A sigh. Tears well. She bites her lip. "Happy, you need help."

"This isn't help."

"They say you were having sex…?"

"You don't know him."

"It's dangerous, Happy," she says. "That kind of thing… it's not okay…you're young. You're confused. Those kinds of things…those feelings…did he make you?" I shake my head. I stand. "Jim seems nice," she says. "He wants to help. Are you going to let him?"

"I have to go," I say.

"Happy," Mom says, "listen…"

I shake my head and open the door. Staff stands on the other side. Mom rises from her chair. "Maybe next Saturday?" she asks.

"Sure."

"Is there…is there anything I can do?"

"Too late," I say.

The tears run over her cheeks.

"I have to go," I say.

She nods, and I walk away. I hate the heavy feeling in my gut. The feeling that I've done something wrong. The feeling that somehow this is all my fault.

❧

Staff walks me through the quiet halls. Things still feel off. Awkward. Everyone's still in school and all of C-Ward seems to echo with the lack of people. When we get to the Commons, Staff gives me a cigarette. I sit on the couch and wait. I have no idea what's coming next. No one tells me anything.

On the other side of the windows, hummingbirds chase each other in the rhodies. The sunlight's bright but the air's a bit chilled. I shiver a little. I hurt a little. I try to figure things out. Everything seemed to change in the meeting, but I can't put my finger on anything specific.

I sit and think broken thoughts until Jim comes for me. "We need to talk," he says.

I stub my cigarette out and stand. Jim takes me to his office and I slump into my usual place. Jim shuffles though papers for a minute. Impatience flashes in the center of my chest.

"About last night," he says, finally. "That kind of thing… we can't have people doing those things on the C-Ward."

"No one got hurt," I say.

"You're children…"

I shake my head. "I'm fourteen."

"Exactly. Fourteen is not old enough. You are not prepared to handle the consequences of your decisions."

"Whatever."

"It's not safe," Jim says, frowning. "You think you know something but you don't. You think this is just something… something you do to…to pass the time. I know it's hard, being around people. Your body's changing—"

"Jesus."

"Listen," he says, "it's not appropriate. It's not okay. I have to talk to Bug's family now..."

"So?"

"I have to explain to them that he is...that the two of you..." He stops for a moment and seems to pick through his words. "I can help you."

"I don't need your help."

"I think you do," Jim says.

I look at the ceiling.

"Happy, your mother's worried...she thinks...she doesn't know what to think. I told her that I would help you through this. I've moved Bug out of your room."

The words punch into me.

"What?"

"I will protect the people here," Jim says. "I cannot force you...I can't make you...but I will not allow you to spread this...this illness..."

"Illness?"

"Yes!" He slams his hand on his desk. The sound of it shocks us both silent. But only for a minute. "Yes," he says again, quieter. "Illness." A redness spreads through his face. "You need to know a few things. You're not to be alone with any other patient."

"What?"

"If I hear...if you repeat this...if it happens again, you will be moved permanently to the Quiet Room."

"Jim—"

"No!" he snaps. "I will not allow you to poison this place."

"You can't."

"I can."

"Jim, please…"

"Give me a reason," he says, "either way. Show me. Either do as I say or not. You choose."

A violence rises in me, but my body won't work. My hands shake so bad they hurt. "Jim…"

Jim turns away then. "Go on," he says.

A swirling feeling fills my head. For a second, I think I'm going to pass out but I don't.

"Go on," Jim says again.

As soon as the door closes behind me, the tears start. Hot and bitter. My nose flows like a busted faucet. My throat ties itself into a knot. I hate it. I'm embarrassed. Down the hall, lunch rages in the Commons. I don't want anyone to see me. I don't want to eat or talk or be around anyone. Getting to my room is impossible. I'll have to get past the Commons with no one seeing me. Not a chance I'm willing to take.

I put my back to the wall and slide to the floor. I press my face to my knees and weep. Silent. Great, shivering sobs. My gut hurts. My hands and shoulders tremble. A ragged loneliness eats away at my insides. All I want is to turn to dust. To disappear. But I can't. The best I can do is hide.

Staff finds me. He comes around the corner and stops. Hard. Stumbling a bit. "Whoa," he says.

I don't even look up.

"Happy?"

I turn away. Ashamed.

"Hey," Staff says, kneeling beside me. He winces. His big

belly folds around his fat thighs. Too many chins hang from a round jaw. Big ears flare under hair an improbable orange color. "What's going on?" He sounds truly concerned. His tone's soft and prying.

"Nothing." It's stupid. I'm all shivering tears and obvious sadness. Anyone with eyes can see that my day is not all sunshine and blowjobs.

"Happy, I can't help if you don't talk to me."

I look up at his wide, freckled face. It's open and kind and I know it's a lie. There's always a secret. A nastiness hidden behind kind eyes. Trust is a bedtime story. Secrets are currency. "I'm fine," I say.

"You're crying."

"So?"

He slides down next to me. Too close. His hips bump mine. Shoulders, too. He just sits there. Silent. He waits and I wait. He doesn't move or ask anything..

After a while, I talk. "You know what happened? Last night?"

Staff sucks in a breath and nods.

"It just happened," I say. "It's not like we planned it."

"God gave us a frontal lobe. Just because we want to, doesn't mean we have to.…I get it, though. You guys are all packed in here. There's nowhere to go and no one else to talk to. Still, you know the rules. You couldn't have thought you'd get away with it."

"We did get away with it," I say. "For a long time."

Staff seems to smile. "Still, he says, "not smart."

"Why's it matter?" I say. "I mean, it's just…you know? Fucking."

"Happy, personally, I don't care. But there are people here with histories. They make poor choices. What if someone gets hurt?"

"We're not kids!"

"You're still young and we have to be careful."

"Stupid."

He did smile then, a real smile. "Yes but true."

I think about that for a moment. But then darker thoughts come. "Am I sick?"

"Sick?" he asks. "Because of last night?"

"Jim says it's an illness."

He frowns. Something angry crowds around his eyes, the corners of his mouth. "Jim has a right to his opinions."

"Right."

There it is. All the Staff follow Jim's lead. They watch and they wait and they get off on controlling things. They all think I'm bent. Dangerous. They all hate me. I can't blame them. I hate me too.

"No," Staff says, "not sick. Stupid. Careless. Not sick."

Staff walks me down the hall. Between me and the world. A wall no one can get through. When we get to my room, Staff looks at me until I look back. Right in the eyes. There's something there. Kindness, maybe. Anger, too, and something else. And all of a sudden, his name flashes through my mind—Patrick.

The room's empty. No sign of Bug. Someone made his bed. Too tight. Too proper for Bug's work. His desk is empty. Walls rise over me. The same walls from yesterday. Harder now somehow. They seem to hold me in. I sigh and an angry sadness wells up. I'm used to Bug. I'm used to his occasional snore at night and his more than occasional fart in his sleep. I'm used to having someone to talk to at night when the lights are dark. I'm used to his warm body. His generous lips. His glorious shoulders.

Gone. All of it. Taken away.

Being powerless is not unfamiliar but it still sucks.

I'm greasy with worry-sweat and fear-sweat. I itch. Again, the shower lacks all comfort. The water's neither hot enough nor powerful enough. It seeps out of the shower head. It slips over me, soft and slow. Still, I sit on the cold tiles and let it cover me. Being naked. Being alone is a comfort. For a while, I pretend I'm somewhere else. I don't have to worry about who watches what or what they can do to me. I pretend I don't have to keep my secrets so tight.

A vast exhaustion rises up and drags at me. Moving slowly, I dry myself and decide to take a nap. I remember my promise to Patrick. A little guilt rises up but I'm worn out and ragged. I need to lie down. I'll eat later.

So, I lay in my bed and pull the blankets to my chin. Thoughts of Jim crowd my head. All the things I'd never say to him push in. Powerful words that only come when Jim isn't there pushing at me. I imagine myself crushing him. I imagine the look on his face when he realizes I'm stronger than I look.

Seamlessly, I slip into a dream of city-sized trees. Gnarled. Knotted. Limbs, wide enough to support heavy traffic, motor and foot, growing in long curves. Leaves larger than the biggest person offer a dim shade. Off in the distance, a mountain, white and black. I rise up and see the tree where

Los Angles used to be. And San Francisco. Portland and Seattle. All of it offers a strange comfort.

I tell myself to keep hold of the dream. I tell myself to wake and make notes. This is a book happening. This can make me famous. Something breaks through the thought. My name. A voice. First, it's just part of the dream. An echo. But then it's real. Still, I fight it. I don't want to open my eyes. I open my eyes. Grumpy. Bug leans in the doorway. Not his usual self. The cockiness and confidence, missing. His grin's a little forced. He looks down the hall. "Are you okay?" he asks. I sit up. "I'm sorry. I really am."

"I believe you."

He picks at his shirt with his fingers. Even sad and worried, he carries a certain beauty. Smooth skin. Hard muscle. A face to capture a thousand painters and give them each a thousand dreams. "They moved me," he says. "I didn't want to go."

"Okay."

"Happy," he says, panicky. "I want to say no. I want…"

"It's okay," I say.

"It's not."

"No, you're right. It's not."

He looks gut-punched. Gray-faced. Wide-eyed. His mouth pops open. He looks at the floor and his hands flutter like he's trying to grab something not there. "I can't do this," he says. He wants me to say something but there are no words. I'm caught up in my head. Things come to me but they refuse to stay still long enough to get hold of. They blast through me, a hurricane. Fear grinds against rage. I press it down, striving for apathy. I school my face.

"People are talking," Bug says.

"Okay."

"They say we're fags."

"Yeah."

"I don't want to be a fag."

"Okay."

"I'm not fag," he says.

"Okay."

Again, he looks down the hall. He looks for anyone close enough to hear. He looks for anyone with the power to hurt him. All he sees is me. "Where I'm from…" Bug says. "In my family…they kill fags."

"Maybe we're already dead," I say. He frowns. "Maybe this is hell. Maybe there's nowhere to go from here."

"What're you talking about?"

A floating feeling fills me. I'm here and not here. I'm in my body and out of it at the same time. It's a drunk feeling. Disjointed. Quivering.

"Nothing," I say, unable to think or move.

"I just want you to know," Bug says, "I tried…but…I can't be your boyfriend."

"Okay."

"Not anymore."

"Okay."

We stand like that for a long time.

"Okay," he says.

"Yep."

He turns away. Stops. He turns back. "I'm sorry."

"Okay."

"We're friends? I want to be friends."

"We're friends," I say.

The words ease something in him. He leaves and I wait for a moment, not sure if I'm a liar or not.

Because I promised Patrick I would eat, I get up. Because Patrick was nice to me when I needed it, I go to the Commons. I'm not hungry. I don't want to spend time with people. But I promised, and I feel like I should at least try.

The Commons is neither empty nor full. People finish their meals. They sit and smoke and talk. A few look up when I come in. A few snicker. A boy whose name escapes me says something that makes everyone around him giggle. I stop and we eye each other like a couple of cats, silent and still. Finally, he looks away. No one wants to fight. Not yet.

"Happy," Pudge says. She sits in her usual place. Alone. I almost turn away. "Happy," she says, "here." She puts her hand on the cushion next to her. Her face is a worried line. I take my tray and settle next to her. The food smells meaty. It smells of gravy and grease. "Sweetie, are you okay?"

"Yeah."

"Totally sucks," she says. "Preacher breaking you two up."

"It's okay."

Pudge shakes her head. Hair flops around her face. "It's not," she says. "Bug's all sick with it. People are saying things…"

I lift the cover from the plate and gag a little. Mashed potatoes. Roast and beans. My gut knots. My hands shake. Slowly, I tear one end of a salt packet open and pour it over the food. Making time.

"It's all so stupid. You weren't hurting anyone."

Slowly, I take a small bite of meat. It isn't bad. A little

stringy but not mushy. It sits on my tongue waiting for me to chew. I have to concentrate. Everything seems too hard. Everything requires me to focus. Nothing's automatic anymore.

Through it all, Pudge talks. She pays no attention to me. All wrapped up in her own outrage. "Preacher thinks he knows things," she says.

Another bite. Beans this time. Leathery and tasteless. I decide I'll leave the rest for the garbage.

"Sweetie," Pudge says, "I am so worried about you. Staff says you had an episode. An episode! Scared the shit out of me. I mean, what the hell is an episode?" She stops then. Tears stand out in her eyes. "I'm sorry. I know you love him."

I shake my head. "I don't believe in love," I say.

"Happy," she says, "it's okay."

I set my tray aside. I can't eat anymore. My system's sufficiently shocked for the day. "Bug broke up with me," I say. Pudge's eyes get wide and white. "He says he can't be a fag. As if you're only a fag when other people say you're a fag. Like, last night he wasn't a fag. Like, being a fag is a bad thing."

"Oh my God," Pudge says.

"Don't."

"That's so shitty," she says.

"I guess."

Pudge grabs my hand and squeezes it hard. The cello calluses are edged and hard. The rough skin feels like it can peel flesh from bone. I find myself wondering about calluses. How long does it take for them to go away? When do things go back to softness?

"Do you hate him now?" she asks.

Hate? I can't get worked up enough to hate anyone. I'm too empty to hate anyone. Hate requires fire, and I'm all ash. Not even an ember.

"I should kick his ass," she says.

"Don't."

Pudge slumps back on the couch. "I hate this."

Patrick comes for my tray. He stands over me.

"I tried," I say.

One of his eyebrows rose. I notice they're so pale they almost completely disappear in his soft white face.

"I just…I can't," I say.

Pudge tries to stand up for me. "He's had a bad day."

"Pudge," Patrick says, "please." His voice is all warning.

I squeeze Pudge's hand and she looks at me. "It's okay," I say. "He's okay." Pudge doesn't look convinced but she closes her mouth.

Patrick doesn't look happy at all. "You promised," he says.

"I know. I tried. Honest."

A bit of a silence. After a bit, he just takes my tray.

Pudge goes to get cigarettes. I'm back on Level One but Patrick slips her an extra cigarette. Pudge smiles at him. Breaking the rules sometimes makes you look stupid. But sometimes, it makes you the one people trust. When Pudge hands me the forbidden smoke, I look up at Patrick and he points at me. His face, all stern again. It's a message. "Try harder," it says. "I like you anyway," it says. "You're worth liking," it says.

Maybe it's weird, but in that moment, Patrick is my best friend.

Staff comes with the bell. Group time. We all line up and Staff counts us. Instead of standing with Pudge and me, Bug waits at the end. Alone. Away from me. Away from Pudge. Everyone watches. They whisper about us. About the fags and their hag.

When Staff finishes counting us, we walk quietly down to the Group Room. We take our seats. Bug sits across the room. I can't help but stare at him. He squirms. He tries hard not to see me, but he has to look up sometimes and when he does, I'm there, waiting. Misery ruins the lines of his perfect face. A puffiness around his eyes makes him look all weepy and weak. Stubble blurs the line of his jaw. His usual goofy grin sags into a thin-lipped grimace.

Staff says my name. "Maybe you can start us off."

I shake my head.

"You've had a rough time lately," Staff says. "Maybe you can tell us how you are."

"I'm fine," I say.

I say it like it's true. But the whole thing makes me nervous. The room's too small and there are no windows. The room smells of sweat and cigarettes. Pudge takes my hand. It helps. A little. Kind of. Across the room, Bug jumps a little, as if someone pinched him.

"I have a question," Jules says.

Everyone goes quiet. Jules never talks. People tend to forget that she's around. Now, though, she's here. She stands out, sharp in a pink shirt and black skirt. No shoes. Socks.

Her hair hangs in a long tail down her back. Even Staff seems surprised.

"Do you believe in forever?" Jules asks.

Staff frowns. "What do you mean?"

Jules looks up at the ceiling, as if there were words there. "I don't know," she says. "You tell us about mindfulness… you know…you tell us to accept things." She stops for a moment and chews on her cuticle. "I just think that accepting things…just letting them happen is kind of weak."

"I don't know about that," Staff says. "Sometimes, you just have to get through the moment."

"What if the moment lasts forever? I mean, we're either alive or dead." Staff starts to interrupt her, but Jules holds up a hand. "According to what you teach, right now is all that matters, right?" Staff looks unsure but willing to listen. "If the right now is all that matters," Jules says, "if this moment goes on forever, then we're both dead and alive. All at the same time."

"Schrödinger's Cat," Pudge whispers.

"I don't know anything about cats," Jules says, shaking her head, "but I know that if this moment, this forever moment, is all there is, then there's no reason to try. I'm either going to be sad forever or happy or lost or confused."

"No," Staff says, "you can be perfect and still try to improve at the same time. Just because two things seem to be opposites doesn't mean they're both not true."

"So, the right now can be both forever and temporary?" Jules asks.

Staff grins. Thrilled, maybe, that Jules is participating and excited that someone understands the shit he's selling.

"So," Jules says, "you can love someone and hate them at the same time?" She looks right at me. A bit of sweat runs over my ribs. My palms itch. Staff looks from me to her. "It's just mean," she says, "to tell us to move on... There is no past and no future, there is only the eternal now."

"Jules," Staff says, leaning forward, "you seem upset."

Jules pays him no attention. The moment passes. She's back to her blankness. She stares at the walls. A long pause before Staff sits back in his chair, looking a little worried. "Anyone else?" he says.

After Group, Staff gives us free time. They count us again, and cut us loose. I charge through the room. I push past people to get to the door. They cuss at me. One boy pushes back. Pudge calls my name, but I ignore her. I need out.

Once in the hall, I stop. Cold. There's nowhere to go. The walls are too thick. The locks on the doors, too solid. I stop and everyone goes past. There's no escape. White anxiety pours through me. I tell myself that I 'll be fine, but it's a lie. I'm not fine. I don't know that I ever will be. I can't remember the last time I felt fine. I can't remember the last time I felt anything but a slow anger. A seething uneasiness. I wait for the world to end, but it doesn't. I tell myself it doesn't matter. Another lie. It matters far too much.

Bug stops in the door and watches me for a second. I want to hurt him but I can't. Everything in me is trapped in a case of cold apathy. It's the only thing keeping me alive. Bug shakes his head and goes down the hall. I watch him go. I want to follow him. I want to touch him. To convince him that we're too good together to let the world tear us apart.

My protective apathy paralyzes me.

Jules and Pudge find me at the same time. The hall's mostly empty now. Several Staff stand a little way away, pretending they aren't paying attention. Pudge takes my hand. Jules stands in front of me. Silent.

"Happy," Pudge says, "what's going on?"

I just shiver.

"Come on," Pudge says.

Jules puts a hand to the center of my chest. "It beats," she says. "Your heart."

I frown. Pudge sighs.

"It still beats," Jules says. "You're not dead yet."

I smile a bitter smile. "Not yet."

"They can't kill you," Jules insists. "You're invincible." Pudge pulls at me. She looks uncomfortable. Jules's hand stays on my chest. "You're going to live forever," she says.

"What's that even mean?" Pudge asks. Jules ignores her. "Come on." Pudge pulls at me again.

Jules smiles and wanders off. It occurs to me that Jules is smarter than the rest of us. She sees things no one else sees. She says things no one else can say. Prophetic things. Uncomfortable things. Hard things.

Pudge wants to go out to the courtyard but Staff says no. She can go. Not me. I'm Level One again. Level One's get no privileges. Staff gives Pudge her cigarette but refuses me. Level One again. Not good. I really need a cigarette. I need something to push the panic rising like a bubbling steam out of my gut.

"Come on," Pudge says.

She takes me to our usual place. I kind of hope Bug will be there. I want him to see me moving on. I want to show him that he can't hurt me. At the same time, though, I'm glad he's not there. I'm not sure I can pull off the whole indifferent thing with him in the same room.

Pudge shares her cigarette with me. It's technically against the rules, but Staff decides not to fight us on it.

"Don't worry," Pudge says, "I have spares in my room."

"Thanks."

"You and me," she says, "we're a team."

I'm not sure what she means but it sounds nice. And a little scary.

At dinner, Pudge convinces me to eat. Not a lot, but some. She separates the meal into manageable portions. The spaghetti noodles are watery and limp. Tasteless. The sauce too thick. Salty and bitter at the same time. I pick at the peas and drink the milk. It takes a long time, but I get enough down that Staff makes a note of it. Pudge goes through both her potion of pudding and mine. She takes a bite and looks at me. "What?"

"Nothing."

Pudge suddenly stops and stares at her plate. "I'm a pig," she says.

"No."

She just shakes her head. She grabs her belly. "Disgusting."

I take her hand. Her eyes meet mine. A little teary. She leans in slowly and kisses me.

"Pudge," Staff says. "Happy. Personal space."

Pudge smiles a glorious smile and goes back to her supper.

After dinner, Pudge and I go to the Meditation Room. For the first time, I notice the smell. Something like cinnamon. Or nutmeg. Light falls through the door in a bright square but the corners of the room are perfectly dim. I sit in a beanbag chair while Pudge goes to her room.

She brings me five cigarettes and three Oxy. She slides onto the beanbag next to me. I chew the pills up. Almost immediately, my nose itches. My fingers seem to stretch out. My legs go tingly. It's both pleasant and not. Familiar though. Comforting.

"Do you think he's thinking about you?" she asks. "Bug, I mean."

"I don't know."

Pudge shifts a little. The beanbag rustles under her. Someone walks by in the hall. We go still. "I think he's miserable," she says, after a bit. "He looks miserable…I hope he's miserable."

When I don't say anything, she looks at me. Light catches her eyes just right. Shadows etch the lines around her nose and jaw. We sit together for a long silent time. The Oxy washes through me. Waiting is suddenly very easy.

"Did you love him?" Pudge asks. "I mean, I loved him. I loved him but it was different."

"And I ruined it."

We sit there for a long time and listen to each other breathe. She reaches out and laces her fingers through mine. Calluses rasp against my skin. At first, it feels like being trapped. I want to pull away. Something like fear but not quite flutters through me. I get a little breathless. But then it gets easier. Warm. Slightly sweaty.

"It's not his fault," I say, "not really. I mean, nothing lasts forever." Pudge shifts in her seat. "Maybe it's supposed to happen this way. Short and fast. Maybe it's supposed to be a flash…" I feel more than see Pudge flinch with something like pain. "Are you okay?"

"I just…I don't know."

I lean my head back against the wall. Thanks to the Oxy, it's softer than it's supposed to be. "The course of true love never did run smooth."

"Pretty."

I smile. "Shakespeare."

"Sexy."

My face catches fire. In a nice way.

The Meditation Room is built such that the noise from the rest of C-Ward only slips in, muddy and muted. The air is a soft, warm hand. At some point, I think maybe I should kiss Pudge again. Just to let her know that I'm still interested in kissing her. I think about it for a long time but do nothing. Everything's under water. Moving requires far too much effort and thought. And I'm not sure what's happening. Good things make me suspicious. Everything's a blur of excitement and worry. I tell myself not to do anything I'd regret. For now, holding her hand's sufficient.

Staff comes in and fumbles for the light switch. When they find it, the entire world explodes. Colors bend and eddy. Walls jump out, pale and hard as bone.

"Pudge," Staff asks, "what's going on?"

Pudge struggles to sit up.

"Just resting," she says.

Staff's face is brittle. "You two know better."

"We were just talking," Pudge says.

"Jim was very clear."

I lift a hand. "We were just talking. Promise."

Staff takes in everything. "You two," Staff says, "are putting me in a bad place."

"Jim didn't say I can't have friends," I say.

Staff pinches the bridge of his nose and looks at the ceiling. "Listen," he says. "Line of sight. Don't give anyone reason to think something's going on."

Pudge hugs herself. "Cool," she says.

"I can't have you two doing this shit," Staff says. He reaches out a hand. I take it and let him pull me to my feet. His palms are dry and soft, nearly powdery. "The Commons or, if you want privacy, sit in the hall."

"Like that's private," Pudge says.

Staff points at her and she steps back. "Private enough," he says.

Pudge mutters something.

"Good," Staff says. "Let's go."

The hall is empty except for Jules and she sits down at the end. Her room's close to the door we use for school and courtyard privileges. She pays us no attention. Something up in one of the ceiling corners holds her eye. Pudge and I sit with our backs to the wall outside my door.

"That girl needs a sandwich," Pudge says.

Jules is talking now. To the air. She points at the door. She throws her hands up and shakes her head.

"I wonder what she sees," I say.

"Does it matter?" Pudge asks.

I think of all the different kinds of crazy in the world. The cutting and the starving. All the voices and weird shit people see. All the little cruelties we turn on each other.

"We fight, you know," I say. Pudge leans in and puts her head on my shoulder. It's awkward and slightly painful. The floor beneath us and the wall behind us are unforgiving. "We fight. We try to fit in." Jules puts her face in her hands. After a moment, she gets up and goes to her room. "I mean, what if we never get out of here? What if this is it? We could all be dead right now...maybe this isn't real...maybe this is all there is, and the only way out...like Curtis."

Pudge reaches up and cups my chin. "Sweetie. Stop."

So, I stop. But the panic doesn't. My heart still rattles in my ribs. My hands still shake. My gut's a ball of wire. The Oxy-numb fades. I clench my teeth and look at the ceiling. Still, tears run hot over my face. I'm becoming a character. I'm the Sad Boy. The Quiet Boy. The Boy Who Cries in Public. It's embarrassing and maddening. I want to be so much more but I don't know how. Much of my life, I spend too much time trying to be something I'm not. Something people like. Failing over and over. I'm the Odd Boy. The Troubled Boy.

"Sweetie," Pudge says, "don't cry." She strokes my hair. Calluses catch a little on the thin strands. They unroll the long curls. I try to swallow a couple of times but my throat's broken.

"The hardest part," I say. "The hardest part is...I don't

know what I want. Sometimes, I think maybe I want this or I want that…then I get it. I get what I think I want—I get Bug. I want him and I get him and for a minute it's nice, really nice, and then it breaks. Bug's not what I want. Every time it happens, I get something and it changes. I change. I become something I'm not, something I don't want to be. There's no dignity. There's no glory. This fight…no matter what I do, there's no way out. We can't win. I think that's what Curtis figured out. I think he figured out that even if we get out of here, if C-Ward goes away, we have to fight for every day. I think he figured out there's only one way out."

"Sweetie," Pudge says, "trust me." She stared at me with hard eyes.

We both know trust isn't part of the game. Trust, like hope, is an illusion. Still, we can pretend.

That night I struggle with sleep. The room is too dark. Too empty. Too quiet. For a long time, I just lie there, waiting for sleep to come. But it's slow and painful. I listen to Staff in the hall talking politics. They seem to disagree on something. But then they laugh and open my door just a bit to do Checks. Light falls over me, but I hold still. I want nothing to do with them.

After a bit, I have to roll from one side to the other and after that, I have to roll back. I try to lie flat. First on my belly. That makes my back hurt. Then on my back, which makes it hard to breathe.

Whenever I close my eyes, jagged thoughts jumble around in my head. Thoughts of Bug, naked. His glorious chest wet from the shower. His hands gentle. Bug standing in the door telling me we can't be together. I think of my dad. The blood in the shower. Mom pulling me away so the paramedics could get to him. I think of Mom at the meeting, looking down at her hands. Jim smacking his desk.

Somehow, I slip into the hollow space between thinking and dreaming. There's music. People. Movement. Voices call my name. They sing songs I can't remember. I need to get somewhere. Fast. But I don't know where or why.

Once or twice, I wake and look for a clock before remembering there are no clocks in C-Ward. Once, in a dream, I stand on the edge of something incomprehensible. Just as I step over and start to fall, my whole body jerks. I sit up before I'm even awake.

I give up and get up. I wait for Staff to do their Checks again before digging a cigarette out of my desk drawer and going to the window. Short bits of chain keep the window from opening more than a couple of inches.

I sit on the ledge and stare out at the night. Lamps in the parking lot outline trees across the lawn. The weather's changed. Rain falls like sand against the window. The tobacco smoke is hard and comforting. Parts of me burn. Other parts ease. My head spins a little and I feel slightly sick. I roll the cigarette back and forth between my thumb and forefinger. I work my way closer to the fire. I'm empty. Everything's distant and surreal. The fire burns dark holes in the pads of my fingers. When the pain gets too bad, I stop and wait for it to fade. Then I do it again.

Sometimes, when I'm quiet enough, I hear the sizzle from where the fire meets the meat. When the cigarette's gone, I light another and start over.

I lose track of time. Staff comes in again for Checks. "Happy," she says. "What're you doing?" I drop the cigarette into the hedge outside the window. "Are you smoking?" Staff says, taking my hand. "You're not supposed to smoke in here." I wince. "What?" I shake my head. She checks my fingers. "Jesus," she says. "Come on."

Staff takes me out the nurses' station, where they wrap my fingers in gauze and ointment; they give me pills to help me sleep.

"You need to go to bed," Staff says.

I don't want sleep. I want another cigarette.

In the morning, Pudge and I sit in our usual spot on the usual couch. I nibble at breakfast. Pudge eats what I can't. It's fascinating. Nature-movie kind of fascinating.

"I don't know how you do it," she says more than once.

"What?"

"If I ate like you eat," she says, "I'd die."

"Sorry," I say.

"Oh, sweetie, don't be sorry."

"Okay."

"It's just a thing," she says.

"A weird thing," I say.

"Yeah," she says, "a weird thing."

Bug comes into the Commons. People stop talking. They watch and wait for things to unfold. Bug stands in the door. Pudge straightens like a threatened cat. She fairly hisses whenever she says his name. "I can't believe that boy."

"What?"

"He seems so cool," she says.

I've reached a certain apathy about the whole thing. Pudge holds a grudge, though. As if Bug's broken up with her. The loyalty is warm but odd. I just want to forget. But Bug is there. Every day. Every time I see him, I remember.

"You're so much better off," Pudge says.

"I don't know."

"Trust me," she says. "I'm a much better girlfriend than him."

Bug eats alone. No one talks to him. They talk about him. They talk about me, too, but I am scarier. I stare at them until the words dry on their tongues. And Pudge is absolutely skilled at tearing people down. Bug, though, tries to shoulder through the gossip in a sullen silence. Nothing makes a better target than someone trying to just live their life.

We go to school. I grunt through Math. Pudge tries to help.

"It's not that hard," she says. "Just pay attention."

I try, and still I write down the wrong numbers or lose my train of thought.

"Just follow the steps," Pudge says. "Step one. Step two."

I shake my head. The hardest part isn't flunking. Grades mean shit to me. The hardest part is the wasted time. Math seems to stretch on and on. Since there are no clocks, there's no telling how long I have left before all the numbers and letters are just another memory.

"Jesus, Happy," Pudge says, over and over. "Focus."

Impossible.

In English, Funk read Hesse to us.

Now I drink pain in every delight
And poison in every wine;
I never knew it would be so bitter
To be alone,
Alone, without you.

He let the end of the poem settle on us. Most of us stare at the walls. Glassy-eyed. Bored.

"Happy," Funk says. I look up. "What do you think?"

"What?" I say. Funk frowns. He likes to think his classes are thrilling. When he runs against our indifference, he always frowns. It's a pained look. "What do you think of the poem?"

"I don't know," I say. "I mean, it's sad."

"Sad?"

"I don't know. It's hard."

Funk's face brightens. Just a little. Someone snickers. For a second, I choke on the words. Standing out carries a certain danger. In the real world, you get to go home after school. In C-Ward, there is no escape. Shit follows you around.

"What's hard?" Funk asks.

He cares not at all for the social dangers. He seems to think of himself as a missionary. His work is God's work. In his own way, he's as bad as Jim.

"Being alone," I say.

People start whispering. Funk spins in place, his face all stern and ridiculous. For the most part, everyone knows he isn't going to do anything. Unless shit gets real deep, Funk never narcs on us. He believes that education requires a certain freedom and that freedom includes having a place to say the impolite and transgressive. He does not, however, tolerate any kind of bullying.

Bug raises his hand. Funk nods at him.

"We're not alone," Bug says. "Not unless we choose to be."

Pudge snorts. Funk points a long finger at her. "Pudge," he says. "Use your words."

"We're all alone," Pudge says, "even when we're together. There's no getting through the walls of our skulls." Bug shakes his head. "The best we can hope for," Pudge continues, "are short periods of connection and even then it's temporary."

"Nothing lasts forever," I say.

Bug stares. I stare back until he looks away. It's like we've just had a fight and, somehow, I've won. Only, I don't feel all that triumphant.

At lunch, Staff lets us sit in the courtyard. It's cooler than usual. Clouds come in from the mountains. Bunched and broken. Slightly dark on the bottom. Last night's rain left the grass wet, the ground a little softer.

Pudge manages to sneak me a smoke. We sit on lawn chairs. Hummingbirds fight over the feeder. Bright and buzzing. A small wind upsets the elm's branches. Leaves flip and wave. The grass is an even green mat. Beatles, black with blue stripes, scuttle around in the dirt between roots. All of it makes me feel small. The trees and the grass, the birds and the clouds go about their business without a thought for my spinning sadness and jagged worry.

I tell myself it doesn't matter. If things are going to go bad, they'll go bad in their own time. Nothing to be gained from worrying.

I eat a little. A dry burger on hard bread. Fries somehow both soggy and hard. Pudge flicks an ant from her arm. She's gone through her own food and now eyes mine.

"You going to eat that?" she asks.

I hand her my tray and watch her eat. It's kind of amazing. It's also kind of amazing that Pudge doesn't weigh five hundred pounds. She clearly has a food thing. I keep my peace though. One thing Pudge can't tolerate is someone pointing out her diet's outrageousness. She gets all weepy and defensive. I have to be careful not to stare too long.

Across the yard, Bug sits at a small plastic table with two girls whose names I should know but don't. They lean in close together. Their noses almost brush against each other as they whisper. They totally ignore Bug. Everything about him is worn and faded. Part of me wants to see his sly grin. Part of me wants to see the confident and cocky boy I thought I loved. Another part of me relishes his misery.

He looks up and catches my eye. For a second, everything goes away. It's just Bug and me. I want to look away but I can't. His eyes are huge and red. Like he's been crying. It's hard to imagine. Crying's a weakness and Bug's anything but weak.

After a second, he stands. I think maybe he's going to come over but he doesn't.

"I've been thinking," Pudge says. "When we get out of here...I've been thinking that maybe we can go somewhere."

"What?"

"I am thinking," she says. "You and me, we can go

somewhere. My mom says New York's pretty cool."

I'm not really paying attention. I'm too wrapped up thinking about what I would say to Bug the next time I saw him. I think maybe I'll tell him to go to hell or maybe I'll forgive him. Pros and cons. I'm more than a little muddled over the whole thing. Bug is my first real boyfriend. My first real break-up. I imagine Jim is more than pleased that Bug and I aren't talking.

"Or San Francisco," Pudge says.

"Okay."

"You can be a poet," she says. "I'll be a dancer."

I blink back to reality. "You dance?"

Pudge smiles and grabs her belly. "If I can lose this tire."

"I like the tire," I say.

Her smile gets sunny and she kisses my cheek. "Dahling," she says, all movie-star voice. "You're too kind."

"Pudge," Staff yells across the yard. "Space!"

Pudge giggles and pulls away. She takes our trays to the cart.

Space, I think. *We all need a little more space.*

Lunch ends. Staff does the bell thing. They do the counting thing. We line up. It's Group time but Jim decides to pull me. No problem. I hate Group. Still, when Jim calls my name an icy dread hardens around my spine.

"Come with me," he says. I follow him to his office. He shuts the door. "Please," he says and waves his hand at the chair.

It's an invitation. But it's more than that. It's a gentle direction. He stands behind his desk, waiting. I almost try to wait him out but Jim's better at the mind games than I am. In the end, I slump into the chair. Uncomfortable and watchful. Jim sits too. "I've been talking to your mother," he says.

"Okay."

"We're worried about you," he says. "This thing with Bug—"

"That's over," I say.

Jim frowns at the interruption. "I'm aware. Still, your mother and I think you have a problem."

He's clearly on a track to something.

"Jim…"

He holds up a hand. Impatient. His bland face hard now. Irritated. "She told me about your father's suicide," he says. Everything in me goes rigid and cold. Jim ignores me. "You suffered a shock. Your father's suicide—"

"Stop!"

The word comes out louder than I intended. Fiery and angry. I don't talk about that. Jim has no business talking about that. Mom has no business telling him. Jim's eyes go a little wide.

"You don't know what you're talking about," I say. "My dad…my dad…he died. It…you don't get to talk about him."

"Happy," Jim says, "let me finish." I shake my head. "You suffered a loss." His face is back to the blandness he seems to think is compassionate and kind. "Your father's suicide—"

"Don't."

"Your father's suicide obviously did something to you," Jim says. "It changed how you see the world." His words pinged into me like stones. "Your mother tells me that she retreated. You were left alone. She says she wasn't there to teach you how to form appropriate connections."

"She works," I say. "She has a job."

"I think," Jim says, "she left you too much alone and you developed some problematic habits and connections. The drugs. The attractions to…the inappropriate attractions." I shake my head. "I can help with that. Your mother's signed off—"

"Help?"

"Your mother wants me to do what I can. There are treatments…treatments designed to repair this kind of illness."

"I'm not sick."

"You're a child."

"I'm fourteen!"

Jim smiles as if I made his point for him. "I'm changing your schedule," he says. "Group is doing you no good. So, instead, you'll come here. Everyday. We'll work together on this…problem."

I swallow. It hurts. "I don't want..."

"But your mother does, and as you say yourself, you're fourteen."

"No," I say.

Jim comes around his desk and leans against it. "Relax," he says. "Everything's going to be fine."

Jim sits on the edge of his desk. Arms and legs crossed. Completely closed off. His unremarkable face is far too focused. Far too hard. Nearly joyful. Wide eyes fix on me. For a long time, he says nothing. My skin stretches tight over every joint and bone. My lips go dry. My tongue seems to swell. Jim is too close. I push my chair back.

"Oh no," he says, grabbing the arms of my chair and pulling me closer. My knees bump his.

I shake my head. "Please."

Jim leans forward a little. Enough to scare me. "Your dad," he says. His voice is too soft. Menacing. Mean. I shake my head. "He died, right?"

For a moment, I feel as if I'm going to puke. I'm going to shit myself. But it passes when Jim leans away. Still, he watches me with hard eyes. I wrap my arms around my gut. It's the only way to keep from falling out of my chair.

"Are you scared?" A taunt. A cruelty. "Happy, do you want to stop?" A mockery. It's a kindness wrapped in wire. Cutting. Vicious. "Tell me," he says. "Tell me about your dad."

Sweat trickles along my spine, slithering around the knobs there. Thick. Hot. "Stop," I say. "You…just stop. You don't know…"

Jim's lip curls. Pale and thin. Sharp. "I know he killed himself." I shake my head. "I know he waited until there was no one around…no one strong enough to stop him."

I palm my face. My fingers are nearly numb. Snot runs from my nose over my lip. I sniffle but it does no good.

"Tell me," Jim says.

I look up at him. Something in his face scares me. He's wound too tight. He leans forward. Fascinated maybe. Waiting, maybe, for me to break.

"You didn't know him," I say.

"I know you," he says. "I know you're looking for something."

I suck in a breath. Deep and rattling. "You know shit."

"I know you're here."

"Not my choice."

He leans back again and turns his head to one side. Tilts it. Looking like a dog trying to figure out something new in its yard. "You're too young to be making these decisions," he says.

"Okay."

I pack as much surrender into the word as possible. If he thinks I'm giving up maybe he'll stop. But Jim's clever. He's good at the whole breaking people down thing.

"You can't know the consequences," he says. "Your dad, though, was no child. He waited until there was no one around to stop him. He knew exactly what he was doing."

Jim rests his hip on the desk again. Never once giving me room to move.

"You're looking for something," he says. "You're confused. I don't blame you. Suicide's a cop-out and you were what? Eleven? You were eleven, and you found your father…it's a mess—"

"Shut up."

"Tell me about your dad. You were eleven, and you did what? Your mother told me the whole thing, but I want to hear it from you."

"She wasn't there," I say.

"You were though, right? You were there for a very long time. And now, you're a kid looking for a man…a man to be the father—"

"Not you," I say.

Again, the tilted head. The considering look. "No," he says. "Not me."

Something like courage swells out of somewhere. "Never

you," I say.

"Do you know what's waiting for you? For people like you? You have no idea how dangerous…do you like being a fag?"

"Don't call me that."

"Why not? Would your dad be proud of his faggish son?"

"Fuck you."

"Your mom," he says, "is scared to death. She knows what can happen to boys like you. She knows how dangerous this can be. She knows—"

"She knows shit."

Jim shakes his head. Jowls jiggle. Sharp teeth flash for a second between his reedy lips. "She knows more than you can imagine," he says. "She knows she failed you. She knows this might be the only chance to save you."

"No."

"She knows I can help you."

"I don't want your help."

"The thing is," he says, "no one cares. You're young, and we'll do what we have to do…"

I push myself back again. Lightning flashes though me. Everything's bright and dangerous and I have to get away. Jim lurches forward. He grabs me and jerks me upright. His face stops right at the tip of my nose.

"First," he says. "We'll work on manners."

I twist and fight but Jim is strong. Too strong. His fingers bruise my arms.

"Let go," I say.

Panic makes me small. Weak. This close, I smell his soap and his sweat. I smell his lunch. I swallow everything down. I put on my most indifferent face. I won. Just a little. I see the point when Jim decides to give up for the day.

"This isn't stopping," he says. "I will never give up."

"Okay."

"Tomorrow then."

"Okay."

Jim lets go and I slump just a little. I stagger back. Just a little. Jim doesn't seem to notice. He turns. He goes around his desk and sits. His face bland again. His eyes disinterested. Snake-ish. His hands busy with papers.

"Go on," he says.

It takes a second for my feet to work. My legs are stiff. Wooden. Nothing makes sense. Silver strings twist and dance in the air between me and the wall. A dizziness, a lot like a really bad drunk on really bad wine, knocks me around as I make my way to the door. I look at Jim one last time. He doesn't even notice. He's already on to something else.

I shut the door gently. More gently than I want. I want to slam things. And break them. I want to punch walls. And people. I want to pitch a perfect fit. But I don't. Even though my throat's a burnt column of bile and my heart's a knot of thorns, I keep it together. Kind of. Thoughts crash around in my head. None of them standing still long enough to get hold of. Each one, a stone ground to sand in an ugly tide of rage and fear.

I shut down my face and jam my trembling fists into my pockets. I lean into the wall, oddly calm. Inside, I'm one step from coming completely apart. All it would take is the right person saying the right thing. On the outside, I'm still.

Distant even. All the shit in me is a secret. I don't have to share it. I don't even want to.

I stand there, fascinated by my new reserve, strangely proud, until the Group Room opens and people fill the hall with their bodies and their voices. Something in me panics. It buzzes and bounces around my chest but it too is distant. People are nothing more than shadows and echoes. They look at me and they talk. They mill around, going here and there in ones and twos and threes. I think about going with them. I think about going to the Commons. But moving seems so unnecessary. So troublesome. The Commons is so far away and I don't want to lose the warm calm I've found.

Pudge is one of the last out of the Group Room. She comes through the door and sees me. Her eyes go wide and her hands flutter around in front of her as she rushes over to me. "Sweetie, you missed Group." I nod, not entirely paying attention. Her eyes somehow go even wider. "Is that a good idea? I mean, with Preacher on your ass?"

I shrug.

"Sweetie, you can't give them...you have to be careful."

"Jim pulled me," I say.

Pudge frowns. "Pulled you?"

I look at her eyes and wonder if they can get any bigger. They seem ready to fall out of her head already. I pull myself slowly back to the conversation. "It seems," I say, "that Preacher Jim has a bit of a hard-on for me." Pudge's eyes narrow and I giggle a little inside at my choice of words. "He thinks he can cure me. He talked my mom into letting him try."

"Cure you?"

"Of my faggishness. Using his word for it."

"No," Pudge says. "But you're not...not entirely. I mean, you—"

I grin a bitter grin. "Doesn't matter. Not to Jim. Faggishness is faggishness."

"Stop saying that."

"It's all dirty," I say. "You know. It's all...it's sin."

Pudge shakes her head. "What're you going to do?"

"I don't know."

"You have to do something." She settles her hand in the center of my chest. "They can't just...there's nothing wrong with you."

"He's the doctor. He can do what he wants."

"No."

"Pudge," I say. "We're kind of stuck here."

"Still..."

I shake my head and push myself away from the wall. The calm I'd had fades into a buzzing static. It leaves me weak and muddled. I take her hand and lace my fingers with hers. She looks down and then up. Her face is back to its usual paleness. I tug her toward the Commons.

"We have to do something," Pudge says, but with all the conviction of someone completely out of options.

At dinner, I make a pyramid of red potatoes and peas. I shred a chicken breast to strings. I eat a bit here and there. Only because Staff watches me. No food, no smokes. Pudge goes through her own meal with a viciousness that concerns me a little. When she scrapes the last bit of food from her tray, she turns to mine. "Happy, you have to eat."

I make a show of putting a piece of potato in my mouth. It tastes flat and bland. Starchy. Pudge shakes her head. "You're going to get sick. Starving yourself."

"I never get sick," I say.

"Here," she says, "let me help." She spears a bit of chicken and chews. She looks nearly frantic. I slide the tray onto her lap. "Go ahead."

She wants to say no. I can see it in her face. She wants to say she's full, but she doesn't know how. I keep my eyes down, like it doesn't matter to me in the slightest whether she eats it or not. After a minute, she goes to work and the food disappears.

Bug comes. He stops in the door for a second. He looks scared. He looks sad. He stands in the door and looks right at me. I look back. Finally, he swallows and crosses the room. He stands right in front of me. Pudge stops eating.

"Hap," Bug says. "Pudge. Can we talk?"

"Okay."

"I've been waiting," he says. "I want to…I'm leaving."

"Leaving?" I ask.

Bug looks around the room. He looks at the ceiling and out the window. "I wanted to talk to you," he says. "Like every second since…since…you know."

"What do you want, Bug?" Pudge asks. The words are hard and sharp. I rest a hand on her knee. She looks at me. Ready to fight. I shake my head and she settles back on the couch and crosses her arms.

"I've been…my mom says it's not safe here," Bug says.

"Oh?" It slips out. Not a word. More breath than anything

else.

"She says there's a place." He looks around. People watch us. Some of them silent. Others whispering.

Pudge leans forward again. "What?" she snaps. People flinch. People look away. Not all of them but most.

"We were friends," Bug says.

"We were more than friends," I say.

"We were family," Pudge says.

Bug closes his eyes. "Dude."

"Don't dude me," I snarl. Bug's face is gray. His hands tremble. "Sorry," I say.

"My mom found this place…a church…in Gresham. They deal with people…like me…people like us."

"Fags," I say. The word seems to punch into him like a fist.

"I just want to say I'm sorry. I didn't…I didn't mean to hurt…anyone."

"Okay," I say.

"Yeah?"

"I hope you figure your shit out," I say.

"Do you hate me now, too?" he asks.

Pudge opens her mouth. Nothing comes out. She closes it and seems to think for a second. She stands and stares right in Bug's face. The two of them standing there like that is hard to watch. The Commons go quiet. Staff moves close. They seem to sense something. Pudge shakes her head and pushes past. Both Bug and I watch her walk into the hall. Bug shakes his head and looks at his feet.

"Take care of yourself," I say.

"Okay."

Bug's mom comes and helps him pack. Pudge and I sit in the hall and watch them stop at the nurses' station. Bug's mom is all hard lines and perfect edges. Bug's a slumped mess next to her. He's silent. He looks down the hall at us while his mom talks to Staff. When she turns and sees me, she grabs Bug's arm and jerks him up straight. Bug looks ashy and wasted.

"Mothers," Pudge says. "The root of all evil."

Staff walks them to the Door to the World. He opens it and I see a hallway just like the one in C-Ward. I see Bug's mom drag him through like a toddler or a misbehaving pet. Staff closes the door.

"He's gone," I say.

"Yeah," Pudge says, putting her head on my shoulder. "Sucks."

"Nothing lasts forever."

"Except us," Pudge says.

She kisses my chin. It's warm and wonderful and temporary.

Part Four

Three days after Bug left, Pudge and I squeeze together on the couch in the Commons. It's far from crowded, but Pudge is all about touch. Her thigh always presses against mine. Or she holds my hand. Sometimes, she strokes my neck or my hair. Calluses catch. Sometimes, it doesn't bother me. Other times, I endure.

We read Corso's *Marriage*. Funk gave it to us.

"It's good," Pudge says.

"Yes," I say.

"Not as good as Ginsberg," she says. "Ginsbergesque. That's the word."

"Only it's not really a word."

"You're a poet," she says. "You can make up words."

"Is that how it works?" I say.

Pudge grins. "Absolutely." I put on a grave face. "So serious," Pudge says.

"I'm a poet," I say. "Seriousness is required."

Pudge laughs and kisses my cheek.

"Pudge!" Staff calls across the room. "PDA."

Pudge laughs again and for a moment, things are perfect.

After lunch, Staff rings the bell. We line up. They count us. We walk in a line to Group. Pudge holds my hand. She squeezes my fingers and lets me go. White anxiety buzzes in my belly. "It's going to be okay," she says.

It's more wish than prediction. She stops in the door and turns to me. They close the door and I'm alone again. I feel like I'm missing something. Singled out. A target.

"Happy," Jim says, standing in the door to his office.

I startle a little, and Jim smiles a little. "How are you?" he asks. I sigh. He frowns. "Can we at least be civil?"

"Why?"

He lays his hand flat on his desk. "I'm trying to help you."

"Okay."

"Do you think this is fun for me?" Jim asks.

"I don't know."

"It's not. This is hard…it's hard for both of us."

"Okay."

"Do you have to be so surly?"

"No."

Another frown. Jim shakes his head and opens a file. He shuffles through several pages. Stops. He squares the edges and looks at me. "I brought something for you." He slides a bible across the table to me. I stare at it without moving. "Go on," he says. I shake my head. "Happy, it's just a book." I press my hands between my knees. "What're you afraid of?" When I don't answer, he pushes the bible closer, and I slide my chair away. "Do you believe in anything?" He leans his elbows on his desk, his face empty, his fingers lacing together, supporting his soft chin. I shake my head. "It must be lonely," he says, "believing in nothing. I find that my faith sustains me."

"I have friends."

"Pudge?" Jim says. "Bug? Your friends are temporary.

They'll leave you someday. In the end, everyone's alone. If you believe in God, if you turn yourself over to Him, He'll be there. He'll stay with you forever. You are never alone if you have faith." My turn to shake my head. "Is it that hard to give up control?" I snort. Jim frowns. "What?"

"Control?" I say. "Really? My life's a series of bells. You people ring the bell and we line up. You count us like sheep. You ring the bell and we eat. You ring the bell and we go to Group, to school. You ring the bell and we go to bed and we get up in the morning."

"No one's making you do any of those things," he says.

"Bullshit!" The word is harder, angrier, than I intended. Fighting with Jim is like chasing water up a hill. Unwinnable. Pointless.

"You can refuse," Jim says. "There are consequences, yes, but you don't have to do anything. We're here to help—"

"You believe that?" I ask.

"Completely," he says.

"How much do you make?" Jim turns his head and looks at me with one eye. "You get paid to come here," I say. "You get to go home. You strip away everything that means anything to me and you get…you go away. I'm always right here. This…this is hell."

"Not hell," Jim says.

"Curtis had it right. There's no dignity in surviving."

"Happy."

"No," I say. "Listen…nothing you do…nothing you say is going to change a thing. You think you're helping…there's no dignity in going on just to go on. You can have your God. As far as I'm concerned, if there is a God, he's a dick. What kind of…how is it okay with you to believe in something with the power to do anything they want…who does nothing… with the power to stop the shit…to change this shit we call reality…who does nothing…"

"I believe in miracles," Jim says. "I've been doing this a long time. I've seen things—"

"I've seen things too," I say.

"I know," he says.

"Why are the things I've seen less valuable than yours?"

"I didn't say that."

"You didn't have to." I stand.

"What're you doing?"

"Free will," I say, going to the door.

"We still have time."

"No," I say, opening the door. "No more time." Jim stands behind his desk, wide-eyed and frowning. I look him in the face. "I'm doing the best I can."

Jules finds me in the Commons. I sit and stare out the window. Rain falls. Water runs in thin ribbons on the glass. I watch a robin in the rhodies. The flowers are bright in the gray light.

"You think I'm crazy," Jules says.

I jump, ready to fight. Ready to throw a punch.

Jules doesn't even notice. "I've been here a long time," she says, sitting on the couch next to me. "I don't expect you to see them."

"See who?" I ask.

"The dead," she says.

I look around the room. Dust hangs in gray light. Nothing.

"You see the dead?"

"It's okay," she says. "They say 'you're good people.'"

"Okay."

"Don't worry. You can't offend them."

"Really?"

"Really."

Jules stands up then and walks away. She disappears through the door and for a second, I wonder if she's real. I wonder if maybe she's just part of my imagination.

Friday night, after dinner, Pudge and I walk. Visitation Day is coming and Pudge feels fat. "My mom," she says, "is going to kill me."

The hall's mostly empty. Except for Jules who sits on the floor outside her room, talking to people only she can see. I've taken to avoiding her. I feel bad about it but listening to her is difficult. She lives in a different world. Talking to her leaves me feeling worn and out of sorts.

"I need your help, Hap," Pudge says. "You have to teach me…you have to show me…" A tear drops from her chin onto her purple sweatshirt. Another quivers there a moment before falling too.

"Hey," I say.

She shakes her head and wipes her nose with the back of her free hand. "How do you do it?" she asks. "The eating, I mean…if I can…you're so...so strong."

I don't know what to say.

"My mom's going to freak. I've gained, like, five pounds this week. She's totally…I don't know what to do."

"Maybe she won't notice."

Pudge jerks her hand out of mine and grabs her belly. "Look," she says. "Look at this. She…you can't help but notice." I'm confused. Helpless. "You don't know what it's like." We walk faster for a moment. "You have to help me."

"I don't know," I say. "What can I do?"

She spins in place. "Fuck!"

Up by the nurses' station, Staff checks us out.

"Pudge," I say.

"Oh, Jesus," she says, scrubbing her head with her fingers, hard enough to make the calluses squeal. "It's not fair. Your mom…your mom doesn't even visit. No one cares what *you* look like." The words knock me to a stop. Pudge stumbles on a few steps before looking up. "You know what I mean." She looks at the floor. "Sorry."

I sigh. "It's okay."

"You know what I mean," she says.

"Yeah."

We walk again. Quiet now. At the end of the hall, Pudge stops and leans against the wall. "She's going to be so pissed," she says, hopelessly. "Sometimes, watching you…I don't know how you do it. Sometimes, it's hard not to hate you."

"I'm sorry."

She looks up at me. "You know what I mean. My mom… she thinks I should be a model. She was a model when she was my age. She thinks…she has all these plans."

"It's going to be okay."

Pudge shakes her head. "You don't understand. When she was my age, my mom was gorgeous."

"You're gorgeous."

She smiles. "Sweetie, you're a bad liar."

"Why would I lie?"

"You want to get laid."

"This is true."

Pudge laughs and kisses my check. "You're a good boy." I shake my head. "It's okay, I won't tell anyone." This time I laugh. "Have you heard from your mom?"

"Total silence."

"Sucks."

"It's just a thing."

Pudge squeezes my hand. "No letters or cards? Nothing?"

"Not a thing."

"I can't believe it."

"We're not close."

"How do you do it?" Pudge asks. I look at her but she won't look back. "You never get excited about anything. Shit happens and you just watch it happen, like it's no big deal… like it doesn't get to you. I mean, Jesus, if I didn't love you so much, I'd kick your ass, just to…you know, just to see what you'd do."

I look at the floor and then I look at her. "It gets to me."

"Yeah?"

"*You* get to me," I say.

Pudge smiles a shy smile. "I do?"

I touch her face. It's still wet and a bit shiny. "You do."

She kisses me then. "Maybe Mom won't notice," she says. "If you're there…maybe she'll be all wrapped up in your awesomeness."

I smile. A weak smile. Insincere and terrified. "My awesomeness?"

Pudge giggles, a little sound. Weak and childish. "Your

awesomeness," she says.

That night, I sleep strangely well. It starts with my routine. A wholly inadequate shower. Brushing my teeth. This time, though, I stop when I see my face in the mirror. Most of the time, I avoid mirrors. They freak me out. My face is never my face. The parts all come apart. The forehead falls forward. Cheekbones rise and float free. The jaw hangs loose. This time, though, it all stays together. Instead of the slightly frightening disembodiment, I recognize myself. It isn't entirely pleasant. I've never considered myself good-looking or even cute. But instead of coming to pieces, I am solid and real.

I stand there for a long time, staring at myself. I run my fingers over the patch of whiskers on my chin. I feel my fingers on my face but it's a little removed. A little like the tail end of Novocain. I drop my hands to the cool sink. I tell myself over and over to look away. To finish getting ready for bed. When I finally manage to get it done, it's like peeling skin from a bad burn.

Out in the room, cold air comes through the window. I think about smoking the last of my stash of cigarettes. But I don't. No need to risk it. I shut the window and crawl into bed. I settle on my side. Instead of lingering, listening for Bug, wrestling with anxious thoughts, I slip almost immediately into a deep and seamless sleep.

All night, I dream. Not the heavy, electric dreams I usually dream. These dreams are warm. My whole body seems to dissolve. I go from place to place effortlessly. I see people and they fill me with an odd light. I am powerful. I am strong.

I am weightless and massive. But then, it ends. I wake in the middle of the dream and it vanishes. I have no memories of it. I haven't moved. I'm relaxed and wide awake.

For a long time, I just lie there. I close my eyes and try to pull up the dream again. I try to fill myself with the dream's buoyancy and calm. It doesn't work. Bit by bit, the real world pushes at me. Little seeds of pain in my hips and my shoulders cut away at the calm, stealing my breath away until I have to get up. The thoughts in my head shatter.

The room's dark. On the window's far side, night thins toward dawn's pearliness. I sit on the edge of the bed. Resentful. Frustrated. My toes ache a little on the cold floor. Slowly, I stand. I have nowhere to go so I spin in a circle. My head is all jumbled up. It takes a second for my body to catch up. When it does, every movement is slow. Deliberate. Cautious as an old man or an experienced drunk. My pants confuse me at first. They weigh more than they should. I feel along the waist until I find the zipper. I try to get into them without sitting. Bad idea. I teeter and almost fall. At the last second, I let go of the pants and stumble around.

"Jesus," I say.

In my head, I play the fall out. I half feel my body hit the floor. I imagine my arm breaking. I rub the scar running along my wrist and remember the look on Mom's face when she saw the wound I'd dug there. I remember the emergency room doctor. His distant face and quick, steady hands. In my head, with my imaginary broken arm, I tell people it was an accident and that wouldn't be a lie. The thought of an honest accident thrills me a little. I lift my leg again, daring gravity to pull me down again. This time, I'll let it happen. But the moment passes.

Even alone, I feel a bit foolish.

In the morning, Staff crashes through the door and stops. I sit on the end of my bed waiting for him. "Oh," he says. "You're up."

"I'm up."

"Okay."

I don't move and Staff watches me for a while. "Happy."

"I'm up."

"Breakfast," he says.

"Okay."

Staff waits a minute.

"I'm okay."

Pudge ambushes me in the hall. I'm not paying attention. Focused on getting to the Commons for my first cigarette. "Dahling!" Pudge shouts. "Visitation Day!"

I jump and fall and smack my head on the doorframe. Hard enough to drop me to my knees. Everything jerks and echoes. My ears hiss. "Fuck!" This pain is real. Nothing like what I had imagined when I imagined myself falling. This pain fills my head with red and black streaks. White and blue flowers bloom and fade and bloom again. Bile floods my mouth. Tears burn my eyes. "Son of a bitch."

Pudge is right there. She grabs at my hands. My head. "Oh, sweetie, I'm sorry. Are you okay? Jesus. I'm sorry."

I push her away. Harder than needed. Blue and silver lightning blinds me. Staff comes. "Back up," he says. "Make room."

Pudge sniffles. "I'm sorry," she says.

Staff kneels next to me. "Hap," he says, "you okay?" I shake my head. Feel sick. "Let's take a look." Staff takes hold of my wrist and peeling my hand away. "A little blood." I pry my eyes open and look at my hand. I can't tell if the jittering edges are my eyes wonking out or my hands trembling. "Can you stand?" Staff asks, pulling me to my feet. "Easy now."

Standing is brutal. Nausea. Swirling lights. Waves of numbness and pain in my face. I wobble. Pudge presses herself to the wall. Pale and shaking. Wide-eyed. "I'm sorry," she says. "Sweetie…are you okay?"

Staff takes my elbow and steers me down the hall. The floor seems to swim beneath me. My feet are far too heavy. "Slow now," he says.

When we get to the nurses' station, Staff finds a chair for me. The rest of the Staff swarm around. Everyone focused but calm. Too calm. The pain gradually goes from sharp to dull. From cutting straight through my skull to a thundering pulse. My eyes throb. Staff parts my hair with steady fingers. Every time he gets near the cut, I wince. "That hurt?" Staff asks.

A nastiness comes to mind, but I leave it sitting on my tongue. I learned a long time ago nurses tolerate no sass. They have a job to do and so do I. Their job is to put things back together. Mine is to let them.

"How're you feeling?" Staff asks.

"What?"

"Look here, please," Staff holds my chin and shines a light in my eyes.

It's unpleasant—the touching and closeness more than

the light. "Good," Staff says. "Looks good."

Pudge comes and leans on the counter. She is watery and worried. "Sweetie," she says. "I'm so sorry. I am…it's Visitation…I was playing."

"He's going to be fine," Staff says.

Pudge just stares at me. Tears gather in her eyes but they don't fall. Blood bubbles in the corner of her mouth. Maybe she bit herself. Maybe it's her own private punishment. I tell her not to worry.

"Are you okay?"

"I'm fine," I say.

"Pudge," Staff says, "go on to breakfast."

Pudge doesn't look ready to listen.

"Go on," I say.

"I can't," Pudge says. "My mom's coming…she's coming to meet you. I told her…she wants to see you."

"Go on," I say again. "I'll be there in a minute." She looks ready to argue. "I promise. As soon as they're done."

Pudge looks up from the couch. An empty breakfast tray sits next to her. Another, mostly empty, sits on her lap. When she sees me, everything stops. A forkful of biscuits hang halfway to her mouth. Her mouth works but nothing comes out. She sets her fork down. She makes room for me.

"It's okay," I say.

"Really?"

"Just a thing."

"I was being goofy."

"I know."

I grab a piece of bacon from the tray. Burnt edges. Bubbles

of fat. Crispy and soft at the same time. One bite is more than enough. Pudge looks like I've punched her. "I kind of ate your breakfast."

"I noticed."

"Are you hungry? I can ask for more."

I shake my head. Stop. I press my fingertips hard into the muscles along the back of my neck. "It's okay," I say.

Pudge sighs. "You're not human," she says.

"Bash my head," I say, "do I not bleed?" Her eyes go round and wild. "Joke."

"Not funny."

"Kind of funny."

"Not at all."

"I think it's funny."

"That's because you're kind of a dick."

She lifts the fork again but I take it from her. "Enough," I say.

Something in her eyes light up. Anger maybe. Nothing pleasant. I stare at her until she relaxes just a hair. She sets the fork down and returns the tray to Staff. She brings back two smokes.

"So," I say, after a bit. "Visitation Day."

Pudge smiles. "Visitation Day."

I take a breath. A worrisome seed starts to unravel. "Do you think your mom will like me?" I ask.

Pudge doesn't look at me. She shakes her head. "Probably not," she says. The seed explodes into a near panic. "She doesn't like most people, but you'll never know it. Mom's kind of a bitch. Just tell her she's pretty. She likes to think she's pretty."

The bell again and the counting. The gathering at the Door to the World. Milling and muttering. Pudge wears a purple dress and black Converse. Her hair is perfect. Her make-up a little overdone. Her nails plain. C-Ward allows no polish. She tries to pull me through the crowd but I drag her back. The backs of things feel safer. Having people between me and the door, between me and Pudge's mom seems like a good idea.

"Sweetie," Pudge says. I nod. Just a bit. More quiver than nod. "Sweetie."

"I'm fine." She actually laughs. "I am," I say, defensive and a little angry.

"What?"

"Nothing."

Families come in two and threes. Mostly. One group of five. They come looking for their broken kids. They pass out hugs and smiles. And I feel sick watching it.

And then, Pudge's mom walks in. She wears the same outfit as Pudge. The same makeup. And the same hair. Only more wrinkles and a viciousness in her smile when she sees Pudge. Things slope a little to one side when she looks at me. It's only a flash before she throws her arms out and charges.

"Pudge!" Even her voice is Pudge's voice, only harder. With a raw edge.

Pudge tucks her chin to her chest just in time for a massive hug. "Mom," she mutters.

The hug is brutal. They rock back and forth. I think of a dog I saw once, killing a rat. Pudge's feet slide a little. When it ends, Pudge is red-faced and a little sweaty. She looks at me, wide-eyed, slumped.

"Mom," she says, "this is Happy. Happy, my mom, Deena."

"Pudge!"

Pudge blushes. "Sorry," she mutters.

Her mom folds her hands in front of her and edges closer. I don't want to, but I step back. "People call me Ding," she says. It's almost a dare. "And you're Happy." Her voice slices through me.

Automatically, my hands form fists. Ding grins.

Everything kind of falls away. Except for Ding. People blur into impressions of movement and color. Except for Ding, who gets sharper. Voices dim into tinny echoes. Except for Ding, her voice is glass-hard.

"Names," Ding says, "are important." She drapes an arm around Pudge's shoulder. A kind of headlock. Violent without throwing punches. Controlling. I don't like it. "Look at Pudge here," she says. "I knew the minute I saw her she'd fight her ass her whole life." Pudge goes yellowish around her lips and looks at the floor. Ding squeezes her neck. "Look at her," Ding says, laughing. "Like she doesn't see it, too."

Ding grins even bigger. She lets Pudge go and comes for me. Both hands reach out. I step back. Ding stops and tilts her head. Cat-like. Predatory. I step back again. But Ding is fast. She grabs my wrists and pulls me close. "You and me, we need to talk." Ding wraps an arm around my neck and reaches for Pudge. "Let's sit," Ding says, pulling us down the hall toward Pudge's room.

"Mom," Pudge says.

"Oh, hush," Ding says.

"We can't."

"Relax," Ding says.

"Hap can't be in my room," Pudge says.

Ding frowns. She looks from Pudge to me. "Pudge, darling, you worry too much."

Ding sits on the bed. Entirely too comfortable. Pudge sits at the desk. I press my spine to the door frame. I run my hand through my hair, a nervous gesture. And I regret it. I wince and hope no one notices. A bit of blood slicks my fingertips.

"Happy," Ding says, "come sit." I shake my head. She laughs. "Sweetie, it's okay." The way she says it kicks me in the chest. *Sweetie.* It's Pudge's word. It's what Pudge calls me. I don't like the way the word sounds in Ding's mouth. "What're you afraid of?" Ding asks.

I shake my head. Ding reaches out for me with nails bright red. Too long. Dangerous-looking. It was the one thing that didn't match Pudge. "Sweetie, we need to talk, and I can't talk to you all the way over there."

"Rules," I say.

Ding sits up straight. Tits out. Pointing right at me like weapons. Her eyes narrow. "Do I look like I worry about rules?" she asks.

"You get to go home," I say.

"What're they going to do?" Ding asks. A bit of silence. "Coward."

"You get to go home," I say again.

Ding looks at me with something like pity. Her grin's completely cruel. "Yes," she says, "I do."

Ding seems to forget all about me. She turns to her

daughter. It's a nasty feeling but I'm grateful. If anyone knows how to deal with Ding, it's Pudge.

"Pudge, darling," Ding says, "how are you? You look positively downtrodden."

Pudge looks up. "I'm fine."

"I like your eyeliner," Ding says. "It fits. You know, not as well as the black we talked about. I mean, look at mine." She lifts hands to frame her face. Completely melodramatic. Details suddenly stand out now. The eyeliner is thicker on one eye. Her blood-colored lipstick smudged a little. Gray roots and fine lines turn the whole thing into a poor performance. Ding looks at me. "I try," she says. "Pudge does her best, but she's not a natural beauty." My lips go numb. "Obviously, she struggles with her weight. I tell her and tell her, it's all about self-control. Portion sizes. Exercise. Sexy is not easy."

"I think she's plenty sexy," I say.

Ding twitches as if I'm a talking toad. But then she turns on her greedy grin. "Of course, you do," she says, her hands waving at me. "You're what? Thirteen?"

"Fourteen," I say.

"Well, okay, fourteen. Happy, you can put lipstick on a pig but it's still a pig."

Pudge's head jerks up. My eyes water. Everything goes kind of gray and blue. I open my mouth but there are no words.

"Happy," Pudge says, "maybe you should go."

"Pudge."

"It's okay."

"Happy," Ding says. "Let's not make this embarrassing. Have some dignity." I turn to go. Ding's brutal voice follows me. "So, what happened to that other boy?"

"Bug," Pudge says. "He's gone."

I walk away and let their voices fade.

Too many people in too little room. Voices. Motion and nerves. I walk without looking. I walk without thinking. Everything spins. I want to be brave. I want to go and punch Ding in the mouth. All of the things I should've said come and go. I'm sweaty and itchy. Disjointed and distracted. I'm weak and sad.

"Happy."

I stop.

"Happy." I turn. Mom. Dressed for work. Black slacks and black shoes. White blouse. Hair in a short ponytail. "Hi."

"Hi."

Mom stands there, wringing her hands hard enough to pop the knuckles. She chews her lip and blinks over and over. "Dr. Jim says…he says I can visit."

"Jim."

"Can we go somewhere?" she asks. "Can we sit?"

I nod. But neither of us moves for a long time. "This way."

"Sparse," Mom says when we get to my room.

When Bug left, he took everything. Bare walls rise around us. His bed lies naked under the window. I don't bother making the room my own. It isn't my room. It's where I sleep. It's where I keep my shit.

Mom spins in small circles. Looking for something.

"Mom."

She stops and looks at me. I sit on the bed. She sits at the desk. She looks at everything but me and then there's nothing else to look at and she has to look at me. The lines around her eyes are deeper now.

"Do you need anything?" she asks. "I can…I can bring things. Something homey. Posters. Something…"

"This isn't my home."

"Okay." She works hard at making things normal. She fails. "I miss you," she says.

Three words. Simple. But hard. They cut through me. "Do you?" Mom blinks. "Did Jim tell you to say that?"

"That's not fair."

"You care about fair?"

Her face gets hard. "What was I supposed to do?" I shake my head. "I was scared," she says. "I'm still…Happy…"

"Okay."

"I'm your mother," she says. "After your father…things got hard."

"You went to work," I say.

"Happy."

"You went to work."

"We had bills… Your father… I needed to do something."

"Okay."

Mom sighs and pinches the bridge of her nose and looks at the ceiling. "I tried," she says. Her voice gets thin. Nearly a whine. "This is hard," she says. "I'm scared... I had to do something. I am…you went away. Happy…you went away."

"I'm right here. You put me here. You put me here and you left...I'm right here, Mom. I'm right here. Always. Right fucking here."

"Happy."

Everything blows wide open. "Right! Fucking! Here!"

"I know!" A weird calm now. A strained quiet. Staff comes to the door. Mom looks ashamed. Embarrassed. "Sorry," she says.

Staff stays for a second, suspicious. I look away.

"Sorry," Mom says.

"Okay," Staff says, and leaves.

Mom turns to the window. She stands and puts her hand on the glass. Even from behind, she seems tired. Slumped. "It's my job to keep you safe. I have to make sure you're okay. You went away and I…I let you because it hurt…I hurt. Everything hurt…"

"Mom. Stop."

She shakes her head. "I can't. I can't stop…I have to keep trying…"

"Mom," I say.

"No!" she says. "Listen."

"No."

"Happy, I need you to listen."

"No."

"Happy, goddammit. I don't know what I'm doing. When your dad…when he died, I lost my cotton-picking mind. I had bills. I had a child. I had you, and you lost your father, and I lost my…I loved him, Happy. I loved him and I loved you…I love you. I had to do something. You were dying. I can't let you…I just can't… someday you'll know. You'll see. If Jim can…if you let him help you."

"Help me?"

"Happy," she says, "let him help you. He knows things. He

knows how to cure you."

"I'm not sick."

"Jim says...he says he can fix these...these urges."

"What if I don't want to?"

"Happy, you're young—" I stand. "Happy?"

"Yeah," I say, going to the door. "Bye, Mom."

"Happy?"

I leave her there.

I find a corner in the Mediation Room. Dark. Quiet. Empty. I slump onto a beanbag. I rest my head against the wall. Everything's wrong. I want to be hollow. I want to be numb. I am both dead and alive. My head hurts where I smashed it. I press my fingers to the bandage. The pain's immediate but temporary—as soon as I stop pressing on the bandage, it fades. The pain becomes a memory. Hazy. Distant. "Shit."

Even alone, the tears embarrass me. My hands shudder. Snot runs. My ears ring. The walls vibrate. I hate being alone, but I hate the thought of company even more.

"Come on," I say. "Come on."

I close my eyes and, somehow, I doze.

Staff's bell wakes me. At first, the sound is simply part of a dream I can't remember. But then it's real. And it ruins sleep's slow, easy feeling.

I stretch. I roll to my feet. I stumble into the wall and stand still, waiting for my feet to come back to me. Out in the hall, people's voices rise. A kind of sad excitement. Visitation Day is done. People move to the Door to the World. Arms wrapped around each other. Laughing. A little teary. They hug their broken kids and slowly go away.

After everyone who can leave has left, I go to the Commons to smoke. Pudge comes and drops down next to me, silent, thick, and slow. It takes a minute, but then she takes my hand. "Hey."

"Hey."

Pudge looks out the window. "Every time. I fall for it every time. I think she'll act normal. She'll be nice. This time."

"It was moderately unpleasant," I say.

"She just doesn't know."

"It's okay," I say. "Not your fault."

"Every time… I should know better."

"Family," I say.

"I'm so, so sorry."

"It's okay."

"It's embarrassing," she says. "She gets this thing where she has to be the center of everything. When I was a kid, I used to tell people I was adopted. I used to think there was a family out there looking for me. I always suspected I was special."

"You are," I say.

Pudge smiles. "You know what I mean."

"Yeah."

"Do you think we'll ever get out of here?" Pudge asks after a bit.

"Someday."

"I worry." She puts one arm around me. "You know. I worry that the world's going to forget about us. I worry that my mom will be the only one to remember me."

"I'll remember," I say.

"Yeah," she says, "but you're here too."

"This is true."

Pudge goes to wash away the makeup she wore only for her mother. "I'll be right back," she says.

"Okay."

"You'll be here?" I look at her. She smiles. "Right."

Twenty minutes later she's back. Slightly soggy. But fresh. She wears gray sweats and flip flops. She slips onto the couch next to me. She takes my hand.

"What?" I ask

She looks at me. "Nothing. It's just…I've grown very…I like you."

"I like you too."

"No," she says. "I like, like you. You know?"

I look at her but she won't look at me. She stares through the window. I look out too. Off in the distance, the Coast Range rises rumpled on the horizon. Clouds roll in from the ocean. Leaves twirl in a breeze I can't feel.

"Me too," I say.

"What do we do?" she asks after a bit.

I shake my head. "I don't know."

"I hate this," she says. "It was easier. Before. You know. I think…"

"It's okay."

"Mom hated Bug too," she says. "She hates anyone… anyone I like. It sucks." She looks at me and touches my face. "So pretty." I look away. "Do you think the universe believes in love?" she asks.

"I don't know."

She squeezes my hand. "I believe," she says, and swallows. "I believe we look for things...we're here for a reason. You and me. We're here because the universe wanted us to meet."

I smile. She sets her head on my shoulder. I'm suddenly exhausted. I close my eyes and let the room buzz around me.

"I had this boyfriend," Pudge says. "My first. He was older, like, twenty. Gorgeous and kind. Whenever he came over Mom kind of lost her mind." I try to interrupt her, but Pudge raises a hand and shakes her head. "I don't blame him," she continues. "Not anymore. I did at first. I blamed him, and I blamed Mom...I blamed everyone. Mom laughed. She said he had a lot to learn. She said it was...it was just a thing."

She kisses my cheek.

"Before my dad left," Pudge says, "he had this shotgun. Mom kept it in her closet. I kind of went wild. I cut Mom's clothes. I cut everything up and I took Dad's shotgun and blasted holes in the walls...the cops...the judge said I had to come here. I think... I think that all of it happened for a reason."

"And I'm that reason?"

"I don't know. It's just nice to think...it's nice to think that maybe this all happened because I was meant to meet you." I don't know what to say so I kiss the top of Pudge's head. "I love you."

"Okay."

She looks up at me. "Happy?"

"Yeah," I say, "me too."

Pudge smiles and snuggles her head against my neck.

At dinner, Pudge clears her tray and half of mine. Watching her is fascinating and horrible all at the same time. When she notices me noticing her, she stops. "What?" I shake my head and look away. "What?"

"Sorry."

She sets her fork on the tray and she set the tray on the couch. "You have no idea," she says.

"I know."

"It's impossible," she says.

"Okay."

Pudge stares at me and for a second, I think maybe she's going to hit me. "I try," she says.

"I know."

"It's not fair," she says.

"Pudge, you're beautiful." She looks at me. "You're sexy." Tears gather. "I love you."

Her eyes get wide and her mouth opens but then she smiles and looks at her lap. "You're just trying to get me to make out with you," she says.

"Absolutely."

She laughs and kisses me.

"Pudge!' Staff shouts.

Pudge laughs again. "Someday," she says.

Everything goes warm and soft.

"Soon," she says.

"Soon?"

Soon, I think. *Soon. Soon. Soon.*

After we smoke our after-dinner smokes, Pudge pulls me from the couch. "Come on," she says.

I don't want to at first, but she insists. Pudge is back to her usual enthusiasm, nearly quivering. When Pudge pours on the charm, no one tells her no.

Staff watches us as we leave the room. They watch us in the hall. They watch when Pudge drags me to her door. I stop. I don't want any more trouble. "Pudge," I say. "What the hell?"

"Hush."

"Pudge."

She leans in close. "Visitation Day," she whispers.

It comes to me. Visitation Day. Presents from Ding. *The woman's good for something*, I think. "Visitation Day," I whisper, a little thrilled.

Pudge grins and disappears into her room. I lean against the wall and try to look calm. I try to feel calm. But I'm not. Pudge comes back and grabs my hand. "Ready?"

"Ready."

We walk together to the Mediation Room. Separate. Awkward and trying hard not to be. Staff watches us. We watch them. We fold ourselves into beanbags. Our feet together. Our hips apart. Our hands far, far apart. Just in case Staff comes.

The Oxy tastes of chalk. It coats my tongue and teeth. My throat. Then it seeps into me and makes everything soft and light. Things slow down and I can think. Thoughts form and melt and form again. It's pleasant.

Pudge reaches across a wide and empty space. She wraps

my fingers with her own. "Nice," she says. Her voice is slow and fuzzy. She asks if I love her.

"What?"

"Do you love me?"

"I'm taken."

"Yes," she says. "Yes, you are."

The next day, in school, Funk starts us on Whitman's "Song of Myself." He stands in the center of the room and claps his hands. He always claps his hands. It's his thing. It's how we know he's ready to start.

"This," he says, "is magic. Old Walt is the father of free verse."

Pudge raises her hand. "What about Baudelaire?"

Funk grins a manic grin. "Perfect!" Pudge gets a look on her face. Smug. Excited. "Baudelaire," Funk says. "Is a prose poet. He kind of started the whole thing, but Whitman makes it magic." A boy across the room snorts. Funk turns. "You have something to say?" The boy looks up from the poem. Funk wears his stern face, which isn't overly stern. With his floral shirt and bowtie, it's a little hard to take him seriously. "Mr. Moreno?"

Moreno's grin is a little mean. "Can we do something other than poetry?"

Funk's face goes completely still. He raises a hand but it stops halfway up. He swallows. Words seem to catch in his gut. "What's the problem?" Funk says. He looks a little hurt. Out of sorts. Poetry is Funk's thing.

"Poetry's so gay," Moreno says.

"Asshole," I say. Funk turns. Thin-lipped. A line runs deep

between his eyes. "What?" I say, defensive. Across the room, Moreno sneers at me. "What?" I say, again. A little belligerent. Moreno tries to stare me down. I'm better at it. I take a chapter from Jim's book and watch him. Without blinking. Everything flat. Everything cold. Moreno looks away. Funk kind of grins. He gives a little nod. Pudge squeezes my hand and kisses my cheek. "Good boy," she says.

Class ends. Staff comes with the bell and we all line up. Funk holds me back. Staff frowns. "I'll bring him along," Funk says. A difficult moment. But then Staff just leaves us there. When she's gone, Funk goes to his desk and looks busy for a while. I wait. More and more awkward.

"Mr. Funk," I say. He holds up his hand. I swallow and look around. A poster catches my eye. A long-haired man, bearded. Gray and wild-looking. "Is that him?"

Funk looks up and smiles. "Whitman," he says. I shake my head. "Kind of intense."

"Not what I pictured," I say.

Funk comes and stands with me. He stands just a little too close. I slide away a bit. "Whitman was a nurse, you know, in the Civil War. Before that, a teacher…they say he was probably gay." I don't know what's happening. Funk seems to be trying to say something.

"'Welcome is every organ and attribute of me, and of any man hearty and clean,'" he says. "'Not an inch nor a particle of an inch is vile, and none shall be less familiar than the rest.'"

He waits and I watch him wait. Not sure what he's getting at.

"'Song of Myself,'" he says after a bit.

"Okay."

"I hear Dr. Jim's been working with you." I watch his face. He wants something. He looks at the door and back to me. "'Not an inch nor a particle of an inch is vile,'" he says again.

"Mr. Funk."

He inches closer. It's uncomfortable and weird. Undignified. "I remember being your age," he says. "It's hard. Being here…it can't be easy."

"Okay."

"I want to help."

"Okay."

I want to go. He goes to his desk again and pulls a file from a pile. "These are good," he says.

"What?" He hands the file to me. Inside, a pile of my poems. Hot blood rushes to my face. "Mr. Funk…"

He holds up a hand. "Why didn't you show them to me?"

"These…these are…private. How? Who?" He looks at the floor. "Mr. Funk?"

He won't look at me. "Pudge," he says, his voice brittle.

"Pudge?"

"Don't be mad."

"Pudge?"

"She...these are too good to sit in a file.'

"They're mine."

He steps away. "It's okay."

"No."

"Happy…"

"No."

"I didn't show anyone." I close the file. "Can I go?"

His chin jerks down. "Sorry," he says. "She was trying to help. Pudge is…you're awfully…you have talent."

"Mr. Funk."

"Yeah," he says. "Yeah."

"Sweetie," Pudge says, standing over me as I sit on the hallway floor. "Sweetie, are you okay?" I can't look at her. Part of me wants to rage. Part of me wants to scream. I'm scared of how angry I am. "Happy?" I hold up the file. Pudge goes still. "Happy," she says. "Let me—"

"They're mine," I say.

"I know."

"You gave them…you gave them to Funk." Her face goes white. "You gave them to Funk."

I hate repeating myself. I hate the wild feeling in my middle. I hate the thoughts filling me. Thoughts of punching Pudge. Yelling at her. Walking away. I hate the thought that I might be stuck here, in C-Ward, a world of secrets and prying eyes, with no one around to stand with. No one to hide with.

"Sweetie…"

"Don't."

Pudge won't look at me. She looks down the hall. She looks at my feet. "I'm sorry."

A long silence before she walks away. I watch her go. I'm mad. Still, it feels like I've missed the chance at something.

I sit alone in the hall. Disconnected. My skin is a wall. Nothing gets through. No one speaks to me. No one looks at me. I'm invisible. I sit too still. Too long. My back aches. My feet go numb. I want to be pissed still. Pudge sold me out. She gave Funk a handle on me. I liked my secrets. I liked knowing things no one else knew. I don't want an audience. Being pissed is exhausting and Pudge is my only friend. They're only poems. They're words on paper. And Funk says they're good. I didn't want an audience but I have one and it feels strangely good. Kind of. Weird too. A little dirty. Oddly sexual.

Staff comes. "Happy. Time to eat."

Everything kind of snapped tight. I look up at her. Blinking, I come back to myself. "What?"

"Lunch."

"Jesus." I push myself to my feet. Slowly. Things wobble and I lean against the wall.

"You okay?"

I make my way to the Commons.

As soon as I see Pudge, I stop. She attacks her lunch with an unusual intensity. She shovels food into her mouth with a viciousness that scares me a little. She doesn't see me and I don't want to say anything. I don't want to interrupt. Instead, I get my tray. But I don't know what to do. I spin in place. Pudge looks up. She sets her fork on the tray. A moment. She watches me cross the room. She watches me sit. "Hi," she says.

"Hi."

Pudge looks away and back again. "Are you okay?" The room is suddenly too warm. Sweat oozes along my spine. "Happy?"

I lift the cover from my lunch. A four-inch sandwich. Shredded steak and melted cheese. Overcooked onions. Soft green peppers on hard-looking bread. "You going to help me with this?" I ask.

Pudge looks from the food to me. She grins a shy grin. "Okay."

Staff takes some of us out to the courtyard. We line up and Staff counts us. They pass out cigarettes. Outside, the heat hits like a hammer. It knocks me to a stop. "Jesus." Breathing hurts. The glare punches through my eyes. I feel sick. Pudge goes all Southern Belle. She flaps her hand in her face like it might actually move the air.

"Lordy, lordy," she says. She finds a patch of shade and sits. "Come here," she says.

I stretch out in the slightly cooler grass and put my head in her lap. Branches arch over us. Leaves cut the glare into patches. Starlings eddy through the white sky in startling currents. I close my eyes. "It's hard," Pudge says.

"What?"

"This." I look up at her. "This," she says again, waving her hand. "It's hard, knowing none of this is real."

I close my eyes and watch red and green worms dance. "It's real," I say.

"You know what I mean," Pudge says. "Someday… someday we'll get out of here. Someday, you'll go home and you'll forget about me."

"No."

"I'll go home. Back to my mom and my life…if you can call it that…I'll go home and you'll go home and the world will go on. This is just a moment…a blip."

"It's real," I say. "I'm real. You're real."

"It's okay," she says. "Nothing lasts forever…it sucks, but… it is what it is. It's hard."

"What do you want me to say?"

She giggles a little. "I don't know." She strokes my hair. "I love you."

"For now," I say.

"Happy!"

I capture her hand and kiss the hard palm. "It's all we have," I say. "Right?"

She sighs. A sad sound. "Right," she says. "Right."

An hour later, I sit in Jim's office. He stares at me with his smile that isn't a smile. I control my face. I give him nothing. "I spoke to your mother," he says. "She's pretty upset." Jim waits for more.

"Yeah."

"You need to talk to your mother, Happy."

"Why?"

"She's trying to help. She came all the way in here to see you."

"Okay."

"She's your mother."

"I'm aware."

Jim shakes his head. "I understand your relationship is hard," he says, "but she's trying…I'm trying."

"Stop."

His eyes go wide. "What?"

"Stop trying."

Jim's eyebrows slam together. "Someday, you'll understand," he says. "If we do this right…someday, you'll have kids…"

"Okay."

"Okay," he says, going through the notes on his desk. He looks up again. "Your dad—"

"No."

He stops and frowns at me. "Your dad…" I shake my head. "We're going to get through this," he says.

"No."

He smiles. A sneer really. "You're not in charge here," he says. I wilt. Just a little. I don't know what time it is, but I know this can't last forever.

❧

Lights out. The bell and the counting. Staff sends us to our rooms. Pudge walks me to my door. She kisses me. "Pudge," Staff calls. "Space!"

I smile at her.

"Be good," she says, slipping me a few Oxy. "Tomorrow."

"Tomorrow."

She walks away and I watch her go.

Later that night, Pudge sneaks in. I'm only half asleep. Dreaming of people with no faces. People with long, clacking fingers. I jump when Pudge crawls into my bed. I nearly throw a punch. "What?"

"Hush." She slides in next to me. Her body is warm and soft against mine. She wears only a long t-shirt.

"Pudge."

"Hush."

I go as silent as possible. Still, my chest rises and falls. My guts gurgle. My toes and fingers curl. My nose itches and wrinkles. Pudge's hand finds my chest. A fingertip draws small circles along the edges of the muscles. Electricity builds and spreads. I twitch and jump. Pudge giggles. "Have you ever done this?" she asks.

"This?"

"Girls." I shake my head. "Really?" she asks. "Wow." Her hand trails over my belly. My dick jerks. Hard, nearly painful. She giggles again. "Come on," she says, pulling me from the bed. The floor's cold against my bare feet. Pudge arranges the pillows to look like I'm alone there. "Come on," she says, and takes me to the bathroom.

It's dark. Darker here than in the bedroom. No windows. No light from the hallway. Pudge kisses me. Her hands startle me. She pulls her t-shirt off and presses herself against me. Even in the dark, her tits are huge. They seem bigger now with nothing between me and them. My hands rise on their own. Flesh gives. Her nipples push back against my palms.

"Pudge."

"Hush."

"No." For some reason, I'm scared.

"Hush," she says. "I've done this before."

My knees tremble. Pudge reaches into my scrubs and grabs my dick. Something hot shoots up my spine. I nearly fall. "Jesus."

Pudge nuzzles my neck. She kisses the line of my collarbone. "So sweet," she says. My stomach is a knot in my throat. Pudge slides my scrubs to my knees. She takes my hand and slides it into her crotch. Moist heat. Sparse hair. "There you go."

For a long time, there's nothing but gentle moans. Quiet,

secret sounds. Her lips find every corner. Her hands stroke every plane. I tell her she is beautiful. She shakes her head. "No," she says.

"Completely," I say.

"Pretty as Bug?"

I kiss her. The muscles in her neck ripple. She rubs me. Her hand is hard and warm and electric. The first time she bites me, I jerk back. I feel my lip tear. "Hey!"

She grinds her tits against me. "Playing," she says. "Make it better?" I taste blood. Another kiss and she licks my lip clean. After that, I ignore the pain. It doesn't matter. I'm done fast, but she keeps going, pulling along until she reaches. We finish up. Bucking. Biting. And clawing. "You made me come," she whispers in my ear. I bury my face in her shoulder to keep her from seeing me blush.

"Sorry."

She kisses me. "You'll get better."

"Really?"

She touches my face. Callused fingertips rasp against my whiskers. "I hope so," she says. Blood rushes hot and thick to my face. "Sorry."

"Hush," she says, kissing me again. "You did fine. Check the way." She crawls around on the floor looking for her shirt. I don't move. "Go on," she says.

I slip out just in time to catch Staff doing Checks. "Happy," he says. "Back to bed."

I swallow. My heart thunders. I go to bed and crawl in. Staff shuts the door.

"Gone?" Pudge whispers.

"Gone."

She creeps out. A darker darkness in the room. She goes to the door and cracks it just a bit. Light etches the lines of her cheeks and chin. Her eyes glitter when she looks at me.

"Sweetie," she says, "it's over. Relax."

I sigh and she slips away.

Part Five

I sit on the couch in the Commons, smoking a cigarette. I sit thinking about Pudge. She's been sick lately. Puking and tired. Moody.

Just before dinner, Staff takes her somewhere. Dinner passes. No Pudge. Staff turns on the TV. *Twilight Zone.* I'm lonely and I'm worried.

When Pudge slams through the door and throws her shoe at me, I don't know what to do. No one does. The room goes completely quiet. All heads turn. Even Staff seems stunned. "Fuck!" Pudge shouts.

I toss her shoe on the floor. She storms to a stop. Staff comes, cautious and worried. Pudge drops down on the couch next to me. "You knocked me up," she says, slightly quieter.

The words punch into me. They make no sense. Not at first. But then my lungs start working again and my brain kicks in. "What?"

She grabs a handful of my hair and pulls me off the couch. "You knocked me up!" she screams in my face. Staff grabs and pulls. I fall. Pudge falls too. We're a pile of twisted limbs. I pry her hand out of my hair. Maybe I even throw a punch. Staff takes me one way. Pudge, the other. Blood trickles through my hair.

"What's your problem?" I shout.

Pudge's face is all white and blotchy. Three Staff hold her.

I put my hands up. All the fight goes out of me. Staff lets go. Sweat soaks my shirt. My hands shiver. A numbness spreads through me. "Pudge," Staff says.

"Fuck you."

"You need to calm down," Staff says. "Pudge. Stop. Stop now."

Other Staff start clearing the room. People grumble and argue on their way out. No one wants trouble. They want to watch but not that much. They've seen enough for the rumors to build. They've seen enough to talk about for a long, long time.

"I'm pregnant."

We sit together in the Mediation Room. Meds slow Pudge's words. She's calm now. Too calm. Staff come and go. They give us room but they watch us too.

"Okay." What else is there to say? I don't know what to think. I don't know what to do.

"It's yours," she says. "I went to the doctor. You know, because I missed my period. They made me piss in the cup and now, well... I'm pregnant."

"Cool."

"Cool?"

"Yeah. Why not?"

"I don't want to be pregnant!" Spit actually flies from her lips.

"Okay."

"I'm already fat!"

"What do you want to do?"

She looks at me for a second. Calm again. Her eyes droop.

She drools just a bit. "I don't know."

Neither of us look at the other. "You can have an abortion," I say.

"What?"

"Sorry."

She throws an elbow into my ribs. "Is that all you can say? Sorry?"

"I'm trying…"

"Bullshit!"

"We have to look at the options."

"Options?" she snorts. "I don't have options. I'm having a baby…"

"If I..."

"What?" she asks, angry again. "If you what? If you can help? If there's anything you can do? You'll be there if I need anything?" She glares at me.

"Never mind."

"I wish."

"Just let me know, okay?"

She drops her head to my shoulder. "Happy," she says, "don't tell anyone about this, okay?"

I nod. Like no one noticed. Like it's not all over C-Ward already.

Staff comes. "Happy," he says, "Pudge needs to rest. Come on." Staff pulls Pudge upright. She wobbles on her feet. "Let's get you to bed."

"Bed," Pudge says.

"Bed."

It takes two Staff to get Pudge moving but when they do

it's like guiding a landslide.

I walk. I drag my fingertips along the wall. I count my steps and I count my breaths. Jules sits on the floor talking to people only she can see. I walk past her three times. She ignores me and I ignore her. That is how things work on C-Ward. If we try hard enough, we can convince ourselves we're alone.

I walk. People watch me but they say nothing. I walk without seeing anything. Everything is familiar to the point of disappearing. I walk without purpose. Everything is automatic. My body acts. My mind plays words and ideas and thoughts over and over.

Pudge is pregnant, I think. *I'm going to be a dad.*

Pudge is pregnant, I think. *We made a baby.*

Jules stops me. She grabs my hand and hauls me to a stop. I look down at her for a second. Things come into focus. Her mismatched eyes. Intense. "Happy," she says.

"Jules."

"You're having a baby," she says.

"Pudge is."

"You too."

"I guess."

Jules looks down the hall. Staff stands in a group. They watch us. They look tired. They look ready to go home. I think about home. I think about Mom and how I'm going to tell her about Pudge. For the first time in a long time, I'm scared. More scared than mad. More scared than empty. What's Mom going to say? What's she going to do?

"Babies have souls," Jules says.

"Jules…"

"They do," she says. "They wait in heaven and when God asks them if they're ready…God asks them if they're ready and they…they come and they get…they choose their parents and sometimes, their parents choose the babies and the babies get born, and sometimes… the parents don't, and the babies…they go back to heaven."

"I don't know about that," I say.

"You have to choose," Jules says. "You have to choose. Babies have souls. They choose. I chose…your baby chose…" Looking down the hall, she asks, "What time is it?"

"What?"

"What time is it?"

"I don't know."

She blinks like she isn't sure what she's seeing. "You scared?" she asks.

I don't say anything at first. She squeezes my hand. "A little," I say. "I guess. I don't know. Why?"

"I don't know," she says. She closes her eyes and presses her face to her knees.

"You okay?"

"I'm hungry," she says. She sighs and looks at the ceiling. "I didn't feel a thing," she says, rubbing her fingers through her hair. "Not till I woke up. But then there was only this kind of pressure, this soreness, you know what I mean?" She stops talking and stares at her fingertips. "It was kind of weird. I figured it was going to hurt, but it didn't. They took me back and put me in a bed. They gave me this shot and everything just went away. It's cool." She brushes something invisible onto the floor. "I went away and when I woke up, it was over. Nothing to it." Tears start down her cheeks. "I don't know," she says. "It was just too easy. One day I am pregnant and the next I am not. Funky."

I reach out and touch a tear on her face. Her skin feels like cold, brittle paper.

❧

Pudge won't talk to me. She hides in her room. She skips school. I ask Staff about her. "She's fine," he says.

"She's pregnant."

"We're aware."

"I'm worried."

Staff pats my shoulder. "You're a good boy," he says.

Jim pulls me aside. His face blotched. He doesn't even try to hide the rage. "Do you know how bad this is?" I cross my arms and keep quiet. "I have to call Pudge's mom. I have to call your mom. What am I supposed to say?"

I shrug. Jim lurches at me. He grabs my shoulders and shakes me hard enough to crack my back. I push him. Hard. He stumbles. I stumble.

"Don't." My voice is cold and thick. "Don't. Ever. Touch. Me."

Jim's eyes go wide. The color in his face spreads like raspberry jam. "Sorry." He goes to his desk and sits. He puts his face in his hands. For a second, I think he's crying. "This is bad," he says. "How…How'd this happen?"

"The usual way."

Jim points at me. It feels kind of good to goad him. Kind of powerful. He sits quietly enough for long enough that I start to think he has forgotten about me. "I want you to stay away from that girl." I shake my head. "Happy," he says. "I'm serious. That girl doesn't understand...that girl—"

"She's pregnant," I say.

"I know."

"With my baby," I say. "My baby, Jim. My kid."

"I know." He thinks and the thoughts seem to bother him. "Stay out of trouble."

A couple days later, Pudge finds me in the Commons. I sit on the couch. Alone. She stops in the door. People go quiet. "Oh," she says. "Come on." It takes a second but then everyone goes back to their own lives.

Pudge looks at me with her chin down. It's too soon for her to show, but I imagine I see it there. The baby. Growing. Spreading out. Her face is puffy. From crying maybe. She's paler than I remember and her eyes sit in dark circles. She chews her fingertips. Slowly. Almost shuffling. "Hey," she says.

"Hey."

We let it hang there for a while. Long enough for people to notice. One by one they go quiet. Talk turns to whispers. Eyes roll in our direction. People wait for a fight. They wait to see hair pulled again or tears shed. They wait for screaming. They get none of that. I pat the couch. The spot she always sits in. Back before things got weird. She waits.

"Come on," I say. She grins a little. She comes. She sits. She takes my hand. "Okay?" she asks. I don't look at her. She takes my cigarette. I smile again.

"What?" she asks. I shake my head. "This?" She holds the cigarette up. I reach for it. She pulls it away, grinning, holding it out over her head. I know better than to fight for it. Pudge has me in reach and weight. When I give up, it steals all the fun. "Sorry."

Pudge hands the cigarette back. She cranes her neck and looks through the window at the trees and the mountains beyond them. The clouds run like old yarn through the sky. "Happy," she says. "I'm sorry." I shrug. "Don't do that," she says. I look at her. "Don't just shrug like it doesn't matter."

"Okay."

"Don't do that either."

"Jesus," I say. "It's okay."

"I'm a bitch."

"Yeah." Pudge punches me in the arm. Hard but not too hard. "You said it."

"You're supposed to argue with me."

"Sorry."

She laughs a little. A nice sound. Pleasant. But then she gets quiet. She chews a fingernail. She won't look at me. "Are you ever scared?" she asks. I almost laugh. "What?" she demands. I shake my head. "It's not funny." I smile anyway. "Happy."

"Sorry."

We sit like that for a bit. Silent. Not looking at each other. "I'm scared," she says. "All of the time." I nod. "You do that, you know. You shut down."

"Sorry."

She sighs and looks at the ceiling. "You shut down and no one can get through," she says. "I need you to pay attention… I need you to talk. Happy, I don't know what to do. Everything's changed. All it takes is a second, a little, tiny bit of time, and now…now, everything's come undone." She shakes her head. "Never mind."

She starts to stand. I almost let her but I can't. I grab her wrist. She jerks a little. "Please," I say. She stops. I pull. Not hard. But enough. "Please."

I don't know what I'm going to say. Thoughts are hard. Words harder. Again, people watch. Pudge notices and gives in. She finally settles next to me again. She waits. I pull things together. "Listen," I say. "I don't know what to do. I'm scared. I'm scared and I'm…I'm confused and I don't know what's going to happen."

Pudge takes my hand. She presses her forehead to my shoulder. "It's okay," she says.

I shake my head. "You don't know that."

"No," she says. "I believe…I have to believe…"

"Believing's not enough. I used to believe that my Dad…I used to believe everything…" I stop. I grab at the words in my head. "Listen. We're having a baby."

"We're having a baby," she says. There's a certain amount of awe in the words. "You and me."

"Our moms…" I begin. Pudge goes still. "I'm scared that I'll be my mother…or worse, my dad. And your mom, Jesus." Pudge laughs a bit. "Someday," I say, "this is going to be a story…something we tell people…something we tell our kid…we have to do this right."

"What's the right thing?" she asks.

I shake my head. "I don't know."

"What's the next thing?" she asks. Again, I don't know. "Scary."

"Yeah."

"Okay," she says, kissing my cheek.

"Yeah," I say. "Okay."

Later, Pudge and I drop a few Oxies in the Mediation Room. The usual thing. But it isn't the usual thing. Not anymore.

"You sure this is a good idea?" I ask. "You know, for the baby?"

Pudge turns angry eyes on me. I close my mouth. I don't know much about babies but I know enough to know getting high probably isn't wise. And I have this thing. A new possessiveness. An attachment. Things are getting big. Bigger than I can wrap my head around. Now, even the little things matter.

"Don't do that," Pudge says.

"What?"

"That. You don't get to tell me what to do."

"I'm not…" Pudge raises a hand. "Okay," I say. "Sorry…I just…I worry."

"It'll be fine."

"How do you know?"

"I just know."

I kind of want to argue. I want to say something. But what? This isn't my ride. "Okay." I float for a while, letting the Oxy wash through and around me. It offers an imperfect silence. Room to think. Things slows down. Thoughts settle one by one. I handle them as they come. No rush. No need to push. If I wait long enough, everything comes to me. I turn my head just in time to catch her rubbing her tits.

"What's it like?" I ask.

"Mmmm?"

"Do you feel different?"

Pudge sighs. "My fucking nipples hurt," she says.

"Really?"

"Like someone running a wire through them."

"Jesus."

"No shit."

I spend a long time thinking about that. Without meaning to, my hand rises. My fingertips pinch my own nipples. Hard. Not hard enough. The Oxy blunts everything.

"What're you doing?" My hand freezes. "Are you…? Seriously?"

"Empathy," I say.

"Fucking creepy." I can't argue with her. Because I'm high, the embarrassment doesn't matter as much. "Stop it."

"Sorry."

"Jesus."

Staff comes and says my name. I wrestle my eyes open. "Sorry," I say. "Nodded off." Pudge mumbles something. No words, just a singsong string of sound.

"Phone," Staff says.

"Phone?"

"Your mom."

"Shit." I'm scared, but I'm high too.

"Let's go," Staff says.

"Okay."

The hall's too bright. Too crowded. Staff brings me to the phone. I hate the phone. I don't want to talk to Mom. I don't want to talk to anyone.

"Go on," Staff says. I shake my head. "It's your mom."

"I know."

"She wants to talk to you."

"I know.

"Go on."

Another second. Staff lifts the phone. Hands it to me. I don't want it but I take it. I slide to the floor. "Mom."

"Jim called."

No hello. No warm up. "Okay."

She sighs. Even through the phone, I can tell she's pissed. Her voice is almost too quiet. "Jesus," she says. "What am I going to do with you?"

"What do you want me to say?"

"Nothing."

"I'm sorry."

"Sorry? You have no idea…Happy…"

"We're going to keep it," I say. "She is, I mean."

"Jesus."

"I'm sorry."

"Stop it."

"Okay."

"This is stupid," she says. "You can't have a kid."

"Seems I can."

"Don't!" Even through the phone, her voice snaps. "You need to get her to change her mind."

"I can't."

"You have to. This kind of thing…this isn't a game. Kids…kids change things. They…when I had you, I had your father…"

"She has me."

"No, she doesn't."

"She does."

A sigh. "Jim thinks I should bring you home."

"No."

"Jim says…"

"Mom. No."

"Happy…"

"No."

"Happy, this isn't up to you."

"Mom. Please."

"You have no idea how hard this will be."

"Please," I say. For a moment, neither of us speak. "You wanted me to make friends."

"Not like this," she says. "This is bad."

I want to have a fit. I want to slam the phone down. Hide in my room. "You locked me up," I say. "You put me in this place and you go home. You forget…you think you know what it's like. Mom, I'm sorry. Maybe I fucked up. Maybe this is going to blow up in my face…but…you have to let me do this. You have to let me try." The line's quiet. Not dead though. This is part of why I hate phones. I can't see what's happening. I can't even begin to guess at what Mom's thinking. "Mom."

"I want to meet her," she says.

"Pudge?"

"Is that her name?"

"That's what we call her."

"I want to meet her."

"Okay."

"Saturday?"

"Fine."

"Saturday then."

"I'll be here."

❧

Routine grinds on, indifferent and meaningless. Come morning, Staff crashes through the door. Only now, I'm up and dressed. Waiting. Sleep has abandoned me to long, worrisome nights. I have so many questions I don't know how to ask. Or who to ask.

Pudge meets me in the hall. No longer as expansive or dramatic. Now, she moves with slow care. As if afraid of falling. Her hair lies limp against her skull. She walks me to breakfast. At breakfast, Pudge eats some. She stops and swallows and breathes. I've seen this before. I've done it. She's trying not to puke. She's trying to pretend this is just another meal.

I wait for her. I owe her. She wouldn't be sick if it weren't for me. She'd be shoveling down the food without thought or worry if we hadn't fucked.

"You okay?" I ask.

"Dahling, I'm grand as a piano," she says. "If you forget the puking and the inability to shit." She looks at my face and almost laughs. "Sorry."

"It's okay."

"I try so hard to be a lady," she says. "Like Mom wants, but I'm just so tired all of the time." She cups her face in her hands. "Look at this," she says, looking at me with fierce eyes. "No make-up. My hair's a mess. You can't tell my mom, she'd be so pissed."

"You're beautiful."

Pudge smiles. "You're sweet." She takes my hand. "Full of shit, but sweet."

"My mom wants to meet you," I say.

Pudge's face goes whiter. A little panicky. "Your mom? Why?"

"It's a mom thing."

"I don't know."

"I met your mom," I say.

"That is different."

"Pudge," I say, "she wants to meet you."

"Jesus."

"I know."

"Shitty titties," she says.

"Sorry."

She sighs and picks at the meal's remains.

"You know," Pudge says after a bit, "I used to think about having kids."

"Yeah?"

"Maybe it's a girl thing," she says. "I always had this suspicion that I would be a good mom…better than my mom, anyway."

"You'll do fine."

"I don't know," she says. "Mom tries. She fails but she tries."

"It's okay." I hold her hand. "I'm right here."

"This is supposed to be a happy thing," she says. "Right? This is supposed to be a party. But no one…Are we making a mistake?"

"I don't know. I don't think so."

"What if we are?" she says. "Mom wants me to…she wants me to kill it."

"It's an option," I say.

"No."

"I don't like it either," I say.

"Someday," Pudge says. "Someday we're going to look back on this…what if they…what if it's genetic? The crazy. What if we're passing it on?" She closes her eyes and clenches her teeth. I've seen this before. I know what it's like to swallow your fear. I know what it's like to chew your lips bloody fighting your tears. "I'm scared," she says.

"Me too."

She looks me in the eye. "Are you?"

"Absolutely."

"What happens if we fuck it up?"

"I don't know."

Tears gather in Pudge's eyes. "I don't want to do this anymore. I'm sick and I'm exhausted. No one tells me…this is not how it's supposed to be."

Staff comes. He kneels in front of us. "Pudge," he says, "you okay?" She hiccups. I squeeze her fingers. She shakes her head. "Pudge, come with me." Staff takes her hand, and all together we stand.

"Happy?" Pudge asks.

"I'll be here." She looks me, her face all swollen. "Right here." Staff takes her to her room. "Right here."

"You know," Jim says, "things are changing."

We're in his office. Everyone else is in school.

"I know."

"I remember when my wife was pregnant with our first," he says.

I know what he's doing—it's a poor attempt at convincing me he understands.

"I remember how powerless I felt," Jim continues. "No matter what I did, she had to go through it. She was the one puking. She was the one whose hips hurt. All I could do was not add to it. All I could do was take care of the little things…the things that made her life just a hair easier." He leans back in his chair but his eyes never leave my face. "Do you think you can do that?"

"I think so."

Jim shakes his head and frowns. "You're a child," he says. "You're too young to do this." He leans forward. His face very focused now. His eyes glitter in the florescent lights. "Someday, you're going to wake up and you're going to find your life has slipped by and all you've done is make more pain. You're going to find that all you've done is hurt people."

I shake my head. "I'm not hurting anyone."

"You're hurting yourself."

"Doesn't count."

Jim slams his hand on his desk. The crack echoes from the empty walls. "Of course, you count!" he half shouts. He swallows a mouthful of air. "Of course, you count." Quietly, I wait. I watch him and he watches me. "I took this job because I wanted to help. I have to believe everyone counts. I have to believe…something." He looks at me and it's horrible. "You challenge me, Happy. Nothing's easy with you."

"What do you want me to say?"

"You're going to be a dad. You're going to have to do things, hard things. Being a parent is hard enough without your special…urges. I'm putting you on something new. Something to help with the impulses."

"I don't want to," I say.

He leans forward. "I didn't ask what you want."

Pudge and I sit in the courtyard. Clouds roll in from the Coast Range, gray and black. Still it's warm and more than a little muggy. Sweat trickles into my eyes. Even my lips taste salty. The cigarette in Pudge's hand quivers. "They're taking me off all my meds," she says.

"Is that good?" I ask.

"I don't know," she says. "They're worried about the baby."

"Okay."

"I'm so tired." She finishes her cigarette and grinds the filter out in the grass. "Sometimes, I forget." I frown at her. She flaps her hand. "I forget that this isn't all there is. I forget that there's a whole other world out there. I forget that I'll have to go home someday." She grabs my hand and pulls me close. "Promise," she says, "if I go, you go."

"Okay."

"Promise," she says. Something makes her voice harsh. Husky. "Promise."

"I promise," I say.

She deflates. "I think I need to lie down." I help her to her feet. "You are such a sweet boy." I blush. "Walk me in?" Together, we make our way to the door. Staff lets us in. At her room, Pudge kisses me. "Later?"

"Later."

"Promise?"

"Promise."

❧

Come Saturday, Pudge and I sit together in the Commons. Waiting. Worried. Pudge is plain as paper. Gray sweats and a stained, gray t-shirt. Slippers. Instead of teasing her hair into its usual mess, she's pulled it back into a tight stub. She smokes slowly. "Mom's going to shit," she says.

"Don't worry about that," I say.

Pudge closes her eyes, as if that'll change what's about to happen. "Jim says she's pretty pissed."

"I can take her," I say.

Pudge actually smiles. "Doubt it," she says. "Mom's pretty mean."

"I can be mean."

Pudge pats my cheek. "No, you can't."

"This is true."

Pudge laughs. A glorious sound, short-lived but brilliant.

Staff rings the bell. The sound of it sets my spine on fire. I want to puke. From the look on her face, Pudge does too. People head for the Door to the World. Everyone but me.

"You have to go," Pudge says.

"I know." I don't move. My feet seem too far away. The room spins. Everything goes black and white.

"I can't go with you," Pudge says.

"I know."

"Go on then." She kisses me. "See you in the room." It sounds more like a sentence than an invitation.

Staff opens the Door to the World. A man comes through. A woman and two kids, ten years old, maybe eleven. Then Mom. She comes in and looks around. It takes her a second to find me. When she does, she stops. I swallow. Fear coats my throat with bile and smoke. Mom blinks. I raise a hand. A foolish gesture. Slowly, Mom comes to me. "Happy," she says.

"Mom."

"Are you okay?"

"I'm fine."

She looks around. People swirl around us. Laughter and conversations wash like a white tide over us. "Where's Pudge?"

"Lying down."

"Is she…?"

"Her mom's coming too," I say. Mom's eyes narrow. "We want to get it done with."

Mom turns to the door just in time see Ding come through.

"Happy!" Ding shouts when she sees me. People turn. Ding grins, soaking up the attention. She wears black. Her hair is huge. Everything about her seems to quiver. I swallow again. "Happy, dahling," Ding says and wraps me in a brutal hug. "You're an absolute sight." She smells of talcum and roses. Mom watches the whole thing with wide eyes.

"Mom," I say, "this is Ding, Pudge's mom. Ding, Bet."

Ding reaches out and grabs Mom's hand and pulls her in close. "So," Ding says, with a thin smile, "you're the root of all this evil."

"I don't know about that," Mom says, pulling away.

"Sweetie," Ding says, "you're going to have to smile if

you're going to get through this. It's the only way." Ding looks around the crowd. "And where's my wayward daughter?"

"Her room," I say.

"Let's go then." She hooks a hand through my arm. I try to pull away but she holds tight.

Mom narrows her eyes. "Okay then," she says.

The walk to Pudge's room is too long. I feel all eyes on us. Even the walls seem to watch. We pass open doors. Families talking. People pretending none of this is real. When we get to Pudge's room, I stop and knock. "Oh, pooh," Ding says, and pushes straight in.

Pudge looks at me. Bleached with fear. I unhook Ding's hand and go sit with Pudge. Her hands tremble. Sweat makes them slick and cool. Ding stands at the foot of the bed. Arms crossed. Mom waits at the door. "Mrs. O'Neill," Pudge says, holding out a hand.

"You're Pudge then," Mom says, coming to the bed and taking Pudge's hand.

Pudge dips her head. "Sorry to meet you like this."

"I've seen you around," Mom says.

"Not a lot of places to hide on C-Ward," Pudge says.

"One or two it seems."

Pudge flinches. Mom shakes her head. "I'm sorry," she says.

Pudge smiles a thin smile. "Sit," she says. "Please."

The whole thing's weird. Everyone tries too hard to be nice. They wrap everything in kindness and quiet words. A ball forms in my throat as Ding sits on the bed's edge and Mom takes the chair from the desk. "Pudge, baby," Ding says, "you look a fright."

"Mom. Please."

Ding shakes her head and waves a hand at her. "I taught you better than this," she says. "You have guests."

A quiet comes over us. Pudge looks down. Tears well. "She looks fine," I say.

Ding turns to look at me. Cruelty shines bright in her eyes. "I don't expect you to understand," she says.

"I understand enough," I say.

The words are harder and sharper than I intended. They hit Ding and she looks at me with something like real anger now. "Sweetie," she sneers, "this is beyond you. Your part's done."

"I don't think that's true," Mom says, her voice thin but clear.

"Let's talk about what happens next," Ding says. "We can worry about trivia later."

Things get thick for a moment. The air seems insufficient

"Mom," I say, "are you okay?" She swallows.

Ding takes everything in. Calculating. But then she grins and turns back to Pudge. "So," Ding says. "Seems the two of you managed, somehow, to screw the pooch." She smiles at her own wordplay. "To put it indelicately."

Mom sighs. She reaches into her purse and brings out a pack of cigarettes.

"Mom," I say, "you can't smoke in here."

Mom goes still. "Really?" she asks.

"Oh, light up, sweetie," Ding says. "We've established that rules and good judgement don't apply to this crowd."

"Do you have to do that?" I ask.

Ding is all false innocence. "Happy," she says, "you need

to relax. Pudge here's all knocked up. Your tension's not good for the baby."

Mom shakes her head and puts the cigarettes away. "How are you feeling?" she asks.

Pudge shrugs. "Tired. Sick."

"I never had morning sickness," Ding says. "I was fit right to the end."

Mom ignores her. "Are they taking care of you?"

"They try," Pudge says.

"And Happy?" Mom asks. "Is he taking care of you?" I open my mouth. Mom holds up a hand. Ding smirks. "I am talking to the girl," Mom says.

Pudge smiles. The first real smile I've seen in days. "He's clueless."

"Hey," I protest.

"But he tries," Pudge goes on, reaching for me. She laces her fingers through mine. "I can't do this without him."

"So, it's true love," Ding says. Mom glares at her. Ding shrugs. "The best thing you two can do is to get that doctor to do something about this before it's too late."

"Mom!" Pudge says.

"What?" Ding glares at Pudge. "You're children. The two of you. You have no idea what this means. I mean, Jesus, look around. This is a nuthouse. Where are you going to put the crib? Who's going to watch the little one when you're off doing whatever it is you do in here?"

"We're going to get out," I say. That startles them. "We're going to get jobs. I will anyway."

Ding actually laughs. A barking sound. Bitter and cruel.

"Happy," Mom says. "You're fourteen."

"So?"

"No one's going to hire a fourteen-year-old boy," she says.

"Someone will."

Mom shakes her head. "It's not even legal."

"See," Ding says, "it's all a tragedy and very, very sad, but the best thing you can is to put this thing away before people get really hurt."

Pudge lifts her chin and looks her mother in the face. "No."

Ding goes completely still. "Excuse me?"

"No," Pudge says, slightly less sure. "We're having a baby. Happy and me. We'll figure something out." Under her makeup, Ding goes pale. Her face turns to stone. Her eyes seem ready to pop from their sockets. "Like it or not, Mom, you don't get to make this decision."

Ding nods. She lifts her hand and checks her nails, like none of this matters. "Okay," she says, standing. "I'm done here. Do what you want. Have the baby. Don't have the baby. Doesn't matter. I'm far too young to be a grandmother anyway."

And then she's gone. Pudge stares at the door for a long time before breaking down. Sobs too big to hold break through her. She falls to her side and curls around her belly. Confusion paralyzes me. Indecision pins me in place. Mom, though, knows what to do. She comes and wraps Pudge in her arms. They rock back and forth. Mom whispers in Pudge's ear. She holds her tight. Pudge buries her face in Mom's chest. For a long time, things go on. Mom and Pudge rocking while I watch. Useless and ashamed.

Pudge pulls herself together. Mom digs a tissue out of her purse. Pudge cleans her face.

"I need a smoke," Mom says.

"Me too," I say.

We walk down to the Commons and claim our couch.

"This is probably a bad idea," Mom says. "They say smoking's bad for babies."

"Please," Pudge says.

Mom passes out smokes. Staff chooses not to see. "Do you know when you're due?"

Pudge lights her cigarette. "Halloween," she says.

"Nice," Mom says. For a while, we smoke. Mom watches people coming and going. "Is this what it's always like?"

"What do you mean?" I say.

Mom's gesture takes in the whole ward. "This," she says. "Everyone choosing not see each other."

"For the most part," I say.

Mom shakes her head. "Weird."

Pudge smiles. "You get used to it," she says.

Mom shakes her head. "Not me." She shakes herself a little. "So, what's the plan? Have you thought about adoption?"

I look at Pudge. She looks at the floor. "I have," Pudge says.

"What?" I say. "No."

Mom puts her hand on my arm. "Listen to her."

Pudge refuses to look at me. She refuses to look at anyone. Something on the floor seems to hold her complete attention. When she speaks again, her voice cracks. "We're kids. Someday…all we have is right here. Right in front of us. There's no future in this. Not for us."

"Pudge," I say, "you said…we're going to keep it."

"Hush," Mom says.

Pudge sucks in smoke and finally looks up. "I love you, Hap," she says, "but someday... I hope we have a someday. I hope that someday we can do this for real." A fist forms in my gut. "Don't be mad."

"I'm not mad," I tell her. From the look on her face, Mom knows it's a lie. She smiles though because it's a lie that needs telling. "Someday," I say.

Pudge finally looks up. "Yeah."

Mom leans in and kisses both of us. "Someday," she says.

Pudge eats half as much in twice the time. Nothing stays down. Every bite's an event. She chews forever. She swallows cautiously. Still, she runs off to the bathroom. When she comes back, her eyes are bloodshot and her hands tremble. "Puking for two."

I worry about her.

"I get it now," she says.

"What?"

"Shocks the system," she says, a small smile playing across her face. "I used to think you were crazy. Now…a little odd, but not crazy." I shake my head. She takes my chin with her fingers. I notice the calluses are softer now. "Don't look so nervous. Everything's okay." She smiles a weak smile. "I'm serious," she says.

"I know."

"Love you," she says. She jiggles my chin. "I. Love. You." I can't help but smile.

Instead of school, Pudge goes back to bed. Pregnancy perk. I try to get Staff to let me stay back. "I'm having a baby," I say.

"Pudge is having a baby," Staff says. "Your part's done."

"She needs me."

"She's fine," Staff says. "Go."

In school, I'm quiet. I zone out. I stare out the window. Funk tries to convince us that letters can be numbers and that numbers can be infinite.

At break, Pudge meets me in the courtyard. "Hey," she says.

"I've been thinking," I say.

"Yeah?"

"We can be a family."

A sadness softens her face. She closes her eyes. "Happy, no."

"Just listen," I say. "Please."

"It won't work," she says. I open my mouth. She presses her fingers to my lips. "I don't want to. Happy it's…it's hard. I don't want…" She puts her head on my shoulder. "This right here. This is all we have."

"I hate it."

"Okay," she says.

"Fucking hate it."

"Hush," she says.

Funk talks about Buddha.

> *All that we are is the result of what we have think.*
> *The mind is everything.*
> *What we think we become."*

- Lord Buddha

"Perception," Funk says, "is reality. Pain is subjective."

"So," I say, "we're all alone."

"Is that bad?" Funk asks.

I look out the window. I think of Pudge. I think of the baby we're having. "Terrifying," I say.

Funk smiles. "'A coward dies a thousand times before his death,'" he says, "'but the valiant taste of death but once.'"

"I'm trying," I say.

"I know," he says. "Are you scared?"

I actually laugh. "Always."

"Why?"

I think for a second. "Because," I say, "this life requires courage. This life pushes and pushes. Shit happens and I don't want to end up a body in a bathtub. I don't want to be alone when I go. I want someone to hold my hand...someone to tell me it's going to be okay. I'm so tired of being alone, but I'm terrified that this...this room...this moment...these faces...this is it. There's a world out there...there are people and things and places. I'm scared that these walls and these people are all there is and I want more. I deserve more."

Everyone stares at me. My face goes all pins and needles.

"Good," Funk says. "Very good."

After school, I find Pudge dozing in the Commons. She lies on her side, taking up the whole couch. She snores small snores. A shining spit stain glitters on her chin. I kneel on the floor next to her.

"Hey," I say. She doesn't move. I lift her wrist and pull a little. "Pudge."

She grunts but she opens her eyes. "Happy?" She sits up. Winces.

"There you are," I say. "You okay?"

"Weird dreams," she says.

"Yeah?"

"I'm in a musical," she says, "but in sign language. I don't know sign language. And there were monkeys."

"Monkeys?"

"They were trying to steal the baby."

"Not good."

She stretches. Her spine cracks. Hearing it makes me a little sick. Staff brings in lunch. "Are you hungry?" All the blood drains from her face. She swallows. Gags a little.

"It's okay," I say and take her hand, stroking the long bones running from her wrist to her knuckles. Scars ripple the flesh there, purplish against the white skin. The shadows seem deeper, darker.

"Sweetie," she says, "I love you."

I look at her. She waits but the words never come. I can't say them. Saying them makes this real, and real things have a habit of going away.

Part Six

All of Pudge's gentle curves turn hard and angular. The baby grinds her down. All her softness fades. Shadows grow in the spaces between bones. The backs of her hands. The dips where her collarbones meet her neck. Her face gets sharp and rigid. Her eyes glitter as if fevered, turn slightly yellow. Her belly swells. Hard and tight.

Sometimes she's sick for days. Then she's back, tired, dark around the eyes, carrying a certain weight that has nothing to do with the baby. She stops talking. She takes a lot of naps. Staff gives her something for the puking but it doesn't work much. Slowly, she turns to a slightly swollen scarecrow.

"Will you sit with me?" she asks. It's barely a voice at all. A ghost of a voice. I sit with her. She leans into me as if I can hold her up and presses my hand to her belly. The baby moves. Kicking and rolling. "Hurts," she says. "Is it supposed to hurt?"

"I don't know."

She clenches her jaw and shifts her body. Makes a face, a grimace. Pinched. I want to pull away but she grabs my wrist. "Don't," she says. "Please…don't move." I don't know what's happening. I don't know what to do. "Sit with me. Just…just sit with me. You'll be there, right? When the baby comes?"

"Absolutely."

"I can't do this alone," she says. "I need you."

"I'll be there."

"Good." Tears flood the little creases where her nose meets her cheeks. She wipes them away with her fingertips.

"Your calluses," I say, "they're gone."

She looks at her fingers. Rubs them together. "It'll get better," she says. "It'll get easier."

"Yeah."

"It has to," she says. "Right? Hap? It has to get better."

"It'll get better."

Pudge looks at me. Narrow-eyed and thin-lipped. "Are you lying to me?"

I smile. "I don't know."

"I am thinking," she says after a while. "About names."

"Names?"

"Don't get excited."

"Why names?"

She lights her cigarette. When she sighs, it's a long, gray sigh. "Babies need names."

"Okay."

"So, I am thinking," she says, "Bell for a boy, Bess for a girl."

"I don't know."

"Babies need names, Happy."

"It's not our baby," I say.

Pudge closes her eyes. "I'm just thinking," she says, "even memories need names."

❧

One morning, about a month later, Pudge isn't waiting for me. Pudge always waits for me. It's what we do. It's how we start our days. "She's sleeping," Staff says. "She needs the rest."

"Is she okay?" I ask.

"She had a rough night."

"A rough night?"

"She's resting now."

"Okay."

Instead of breakfast, I walk. I walk from one end of the ward to the other. I walk around people. I count my steps. I count each breath. I listen to my heartbeat. I feel heavy and weak. Everything feels soggy and soft. Bending and swaying. Something like a thorn catches in my throat. The waiting and the walking etches the edges of my bones. When I can't wait anymore, I knock on her door. Hard. I call her name. No answer. I knock again before opening the door.

Pudge lies curled in her bed, covered with vomit. Rocking slightly and sobbing. Quietly. Her hands press hard to her rounded belly. It's brutal and frightening. I stand for a long minute trying to figure out what to do.

"Pudge."

She doesn't answer.

"Pudge, what…can I help?"

One hand rises, vaguely purple in the dim light. I turn and call down the hall.

Staff comes, slowly, frowning. "Shit," someone says. They get busy. People rush in. I go with them. Pudge looks up at me. Swollen eyes. Dry, cracked lips. Barely human. It hurts to look at her.

"Happy," she says, her voice breaking. "I'm sorry. It's not

my fault. I tried. I'm sorry."

"It's okay," I say. "It's okay."

Staff pushes me back.

"Something's wrong with the baby," Pudge says.

"Hap," Staff says, "get out. Go...give us room."

I retreat to the door.

"Hap," Pudge says. "Hap. Tell me something. You promised. You said you'd be there." All my joints go solid. I nearly topple. "You promised." They bring in a stretcher. They lift her up. Pudge reaches for me as they pass. She grabs my shirt. "You promised," she says. "Promised."

But then she's gone. Down the hall. Through the Door to the World.

I wait. Minutes flow into hours. I sit in the Commons and wait. Jules comes and sits with me. She takes my hand. "It's happening," she says. I try to pull away. "Stop it," she says. "Baby's coming." I rock a little. "You feel different?"

"Scared."

She smiles. "Are you ready?"

"It's too soon," I say.

"Things come when they come."

She looks into the corner and her face changes. "Get ready," she says. "Shit's getting real."

And then she's gone.

I try to walk but every step throbs in my head. My knees twitch. I feel sick. Everything wobbles and spins. A buzzing whiteness pushes in. I sneak into Pudge's room. For a long time, I stand and take things in. Her bed. Her desk with no photos. A stack of poems. Mine. Ferlinghetti. Hers. Bell and Laux. Kumunyakaa. I find a small drawing. Rough. Pencil on lined paper. In her top drawer, I find an envelope. Oxy. The last of her stash. It's cheap and petty but I take it. Down three. Save two.

I go to the Mediation Room and sit in the dark. The Oxy knocks the ends off things. My ribs open up. My lungs fill and my heart lies almost still against my spine.

For the first time in a long time, I think of cutting. Had I a razor or a knife or even a piece of broken glass, I'd open myself up proper. I press my thumbnail into my wrist. Hard. Deep. Not enough to break the skin. Just enough to leave a thin, white line. It hurts just enough to remind me of cutting's nearly opiate high. It hurts just enough to remind me that physical pain is small and finite. It reminds me that the shit in my head is so much bigger. So big it cores me out. Leaves me limp.

I sit in the darkness until Jim finds me. He stands, tall and dark, in the doorway. Light from the hall lights one ear. Glows in the stubble along his jaw. He looks bigger than he actually is.

"Happy," he says, coming closer. "Do you mind?"

Without waiting for an answer, he lowers himself down next to me. Too close. His shoulder bumps into mine. I slide away just a bit. Jim doesn't seem to notice.

"How are you?" Jim asks. I shake my head. "Scared?" I don't answer. I don't want to look at him. The Oxy still softens things but not enough. "She had the baby," he says. Now, I look at him. "A little girl."

"A girl?"

Jim looks out the door. "Do you want to see her?"

I nod.

"Come on then," he says.

Nothing in the hall's changed. The walls are still the walls. People still sit in small groups. Whispering. Laughing. Staff still does Checks. The light's still soft and shadowless. Jim takes me to the nurses' station. He talks to Staff. I wait, trembling, feeling sick.

"Ready?" Jim asks. I don't know what to say. "Okay then, here we go."

When the Door to the World buzzes, my gut falls. Everything gets thin. I've not been in the World for months. I'm used to walls and fences and Staff ringing their bell, telling me where to go and when to go there.

"Coming?" Jim asks. Picking up one foot and then the other, I walk through. Jim follows. The Door to the World closes with a solid thump. I jump a little. "You okay?"

"Let's go," I say.

People work in offices. They wear suits and dresses. They're the invisible faces running C-Ward. When we cross through the glass doors into the parking lot, I suck in a big breath. This is a world I've forgotten. Traffic hums. Grass grows in perfect squares and trees stand twisted, naked in the gray light. A small rain whispers. Summer's passed. Winter's here.

"Stay close," Jim says, leading me through the parking lot to the street. Cars go to places I can't even begin to guess. People walk. "It's just down the street."

The sidewalk's dark and wet. We walk silently, Jim a step ahead of me. "Keep up," he says.

I bring myself level with him. This part of Portland is all evergreens and naked oaks. The street empties into another. We turn the corner and the hospital stands there. Pale, lots of glass. I think back to Bruce bringing me here and wonder how I missed it. It stands solid. A collection of huge blocks broken here and there with bridges, a portico and doors. In the parking lot, a couple of ambulances. Cops cars. People coming and going. I know they can't possibly know who I am or why I'm here. Still, a small panic blooms in my chest.

"It's okay," Jim says, like he knows what I'm thinking.

Glass doors slide open and we're inside. It's drier here but still a little cold. The floor's all hard marble. Columns hold the ceiling up. We cross the lobby to a bank of shining elevators.

"This is not going to be easy," Jim says. For the first time, he seems human. "Are you ready? It might get rough."

"I know rough."

"Not like this," he says. "This…this is going to be bad."

"Okay."

He looks sad. He presses the button.

Pudge's room is the color of cold flesh. Her bed is rigid. Once round cheeks are hollowed now. Her jaw's a hard line. Both her nose and chin are wedges. Sharp. Everything about her is empty and tissue paper pale. She's a sliver of herself. Under the antiseptic, I smell piss and sweat. Vomit.

"What happened?"

"Complications. She lost a lot of blood."

"Can I touch her?" I ask.

"Sure."

Pudge's hand is cold. Lightly blue. Bruises bloom along her forearms, the backs of her hand. Even sleeping, pain writes a story in her face. It hurts to look at her. "Is there anything…?" I say. "What can I do?"

"Pray," Jim says.

"Pray?"

"It's all in God's hands now."

I shake my head.

"Happy," Jim says later, "it's time to see your daughter." The word hammers me like a bullet. *Daughter*. I have a kid. A baby girl. "This way."

Gently, I lay Pudge's hand on her belly. She snores once. Chews her lip. I hate the thought of leaving her. What if she wakes? What if something happens? I have to go though. I have to see my kid.

"This way," Jim repeats.

Nothing prepares me for the nursery. It's two floors up and in a different wing. Jim walks with me. He doesn't look at me but he's watching out of the corners of his eyes. A heavy sadness sits hard on me. Everything's thick and soft. Muddy.

"This is it," Jim says.

A huge window opens onto a stark room. Bassinettes stand in two rows. Tubes run here and there. Babies, most of them no bigger than a thought, lie too still in the hard light.

"There she is," Jim says. "Last one on the left."

I get close to the window but the angle's wrong. All I can

see are tiny feet. A patch of red hair. A small arm. A tent stands over the crib. A tag on the end of the bassinette reads *Graf.*

"Graf?"

Jim looks a little shocked. "Pudge's last name," he says. "You don't know her name?"

"It never came up."

"Good Lord."

I ignore him.

"Do you think," I say, "do you think they'd let me in? Can I…can I hold her?"

Jim shakes his head. "Not today."

"Okay." I rest my forehead on the cool glass. "She's not going to make it," I say, "is she? She's going to die." Jim puts a hand on my shoulder. I let him. For some reason, it feels good.

Back in Pudge's room, I stand at the window. It overlooks a parking structure. In the distance, the West Hills rise, bristling with evergreens, into a sky cluttered with dark clouds. A highway runs like a gray ribbon. Finally, Pudge stirs. Hope flares. I turn to her bed. Even Jim stands straighter.

"Hey," I say.

Pudge blinks and frowns. She winces when she moves. "Happy," she says. Hearing her say my name is a special joy. Even if it's slurred with meds and fatigue. "Hurts." I look at Jim. He steps out into the hall. "Jesus," Pudge says.

"You're okay."

She blinks at me. "Water," she says. I bring a plastic cup from the bathroom. She sips and hands it back, then reaches for me, but the IV snags. "Is the baby okay?" I swallow air and nerves. "Happy?" I look at the bed. The floor. I look at the walls. I look at anything but her. "Oh God."

"She came too early."

Jim brings a nurse.

"It hurts," Pudge says.

"I'll get something for that," the nurse says, and checks the lines running into Pudge's arm. "Hold tight. I'll be right back."

With the nurse gone, Pudge closes her eyes. She breathes and makes a fist. "Is the baby dead?"

"Not yet."

She stares at the ceiling. "Okay." She sucks air through her teeth. She turns to stone.

"Pudge," I say. She shakes her head. I go quiet.

The nurse comes with the pain meds. "This'll make you tired," she says.

"I'm already tired."

The nurse shakes her head. "I know," she says. "Everything's going to be okay." She speaks with confidence. Pudge glares, but the nurse doesn't see it. She's too busy pumping drugs into plastic tubing. The meds hit hard and fast. Pudge sighs. The nurse looks at me. "Maybe you should come back later."

Jim steps forward. "It's time."

Already, Pudge is floating away. I lean in and kiss her cheek. The flesh there is thin and dry.

"I'll be back," I say.

Slowly, I let her hand go. "Happy," she says. I stop. Pudge opens her eyes just a sliver. "Bess. Her name is Bess."

"Okay."

She turns away then. Into heavy sleep. She lets go a big breath. Everything about slumps a little.

Together, Jim and I walk back to C-Ward. I watch some TV. All night, I tell myself things are different. I have a kid. I'm a dad. Being a dad, though, only feels like I'm into something too big to understand. Too big to handle. I wonder if my dad felt this way. If this was why he put a bullet in his head.

Days pass. The doctors keep Bess but they send Pudge back to us. She wobbles into the Commons. Almost unrecognizable. Thin. Weak-looking. She wears gray sweats and moves with an ancient caution. I stand.

"Hey," Pudge says.

"Pudge."

Staff looks up. "Can I have a smoke?" Pudge asks. Staff hands her a cigarette.

"Come on." I hold out a hand. Pudge reaches for me. Her hand is light and leaf-thin. I lead her to the couch. "You're back."

She smiles. Her joints seem watery. Barely able to hold her. She lights up and sighs. "Nice," she says. She looks at me. Her face gets grave. "Sweetie, you look absolutely tattered."

I ignore her. "You okay?" I ask.

"They told me to take it slow."

"Yeah."

"I don't know what that means, really," she says. "Not much happens fast on C-Ward."

Everyone watches us. Pudge more than me. She carries a certain celebrity. Getting pregnant and then getting sick. The baby coming too soon. People on C-Ward tend toward morbid curiosity. For the moment, Pudge is a goddess. And I am her high priest.

"Tell me what you've been doing," she says. "You look so tired."

I shake my head. "Thinking, mostly." She tilts her head and looks at me a little sideways. "You know, trying to figure shit out," I say.

"Lots of shit," she says.

"Too much."

We smoke together for a while. Quietly. Even talking, it seems, exhausts her. Staff gives us space but they never take their eyes off us. With all the shit Pudge and I've brought down on C-Ward, trust is precious. Too precious to waste on us unnecessarily.

"Did you see her?" I ask.

Pudge shakes her head. "No. I can't…it's too much."

"I thought—"

"I changed my mind," she says, defensive.

"Okay."

"I need to lie down."

I help her to her feet. She leans into me. Staff comes to help. "I got it," I say.

Still, they walk us down the hall. Pudge weighs nearly nothing on my arm. When we get to her door, we stop. She kisses me then.

"Space," Staff says. Both Pudge and I look at her. She looks at the floor. "Sorry. Habit."

Pudge grabs my face with both hands. "Sweetie, I'm okay. Take a nap. Something. You look like shit."

"Okay."

She turns away. Stops. She turns back. "Do you regret it?"

"Absolutely not."

Tears gather. One falls from her chin to her shirt. A dark drop. "Okay," she says.

"Good."

One of her hands rises in a wave. Staff reaches past me to close the door. "Are you okay?" he asks.

I shake my head.

❧

Every day, while everyone else goes to Group, Jim walks me to the hospital to spend an hour with Bess. I invite Pudge but she won't come. "Don't you want to see her?"

"I saw her," Pudge says, "when she was born. I was there. I even held her for a minute before they took her away."

Jealousy flashes through me. I'd never held Bess. I've never been in the same room with her. "She's our daughter," I say.

Pudge shakes her head. "No," she says. "She's a memory. A regret."

"Not a regret."

"We fought the fight," Pudge says. "We lost."

"Not yet," I say. "She's still here."

"Not really," she says. "She doesn't know us. She doesn't know what's going on. You're holding on for your own purposes, Happy. It's not fair. Not to her. Or me. Or you."

"I can't just walk away," I say.

"Okay." "I want... I want to remember her."

"Go on then. Just...leave me out of it."

"I'm sorry."

She smiles at me and touches my face. "I'm not mad," she says. "Not at you."

"Really?"

"For sure," she says. "I just…I can't do it."

"Okay."

"Happy," she says, "be careful. It's going to hurt when… when it happens."

I know about pain. I know about death.

"You're a good boy," she says.

I leave her there, staring out the window, looking nothing like the girl I'd fallen for.

Jim walks with me but we don't talk. The world is loud around us. Traffic. Rain. Branches groaning in the wind coming in from the Coast Range. He has no more questions. No more lessons for me. Every day, the walk is longer. Heavier. Colder.

A week passes. The silence is too much.

"Can I ask you something?" Jim looks at me, his face bland. No curiosity. Nothing. "Why are you doing this?"

He smiles a small smile. "It's the right thing."

"How do you figure?"

He shrugs.

"I thought you hated me," I say.

Another smile. This one clinical. "I don't hate you," he says. "Your life's been hard. You make poor choices. But they're your choices. Your mother hired me to help you make better ones."

"Is that all this is? A job?"

He shakes his head. "I'm trying to help. Hopefully, at the end of things, I'll have done more good than bad."

More walking. A slice of silence.

"You believe in God," I say. Jim nods. "You believe God is good?"

"He is."

I try to find the words. They slither around in the back of my throat. "Okay. If He's good, why does he do things like this?"

Jim's brows meet and he looks at me sideways. "This isn't God," he says. "This is all you."

"And you think it's a sin?"

"I do."

"Are you're trying to teach me something?"

"No," he says, "I'm not trying to teach you anything. I'm just the vessel. Whatever lessons you learn from this are God's."

I snort.

"Do you know what a miracle is?" Jim asks.

I shake my head.

"It's God saying, 'I love you anyway.'"

"I don't believe in miracles," I say.

"I know," Jim says.

I stand at the glass and watch the nurses move from baby to baby. They'd put a tube down Bess's throat. I ask Jim if she's in pain.

"It's hard to tell," he says.

"It looks like it hurts."

"Yes," he says, "it does."

"She's dying," I say.

The nurses do magical, medical things. They never look at us. We're invisible. They're focused on the cribs and the tubes. They move with indifferent briskness. It bothers me.

"I want her to get better," I say.

"Happy," Jim says.

I hold up a hand. He stops. "I know."

"This is nothing like your dad," he says.

"This is harder."

"Yes, it is."

"Do you know any dead people?" I ask, after a while.

"A couple," Jim says grimly.

"Babies?"

He shakes his head.

"So, you have no idea," I say.

"I have an idea."

"Not really," I say.

"No. Not really."

I watch Bess's small, bony chest rise and fall. "Can I ask a favor?" Jim looks at me. "Will you pray for her?" Jim frowns. "If there's a God, maybe He'll listen to you."

"He'll listen to you, too."

I shake my head. "He hasn't so far."

Back on C-Ward, Pudge and I sit on the couch. She still isn't eating. She smokes and she stares out the window. Sometimes, she touches the glass with her fingertips. She skips school and Group. No one says anything. She's too brittle to touch. She fades into the couch. She twitches and shivers. She whimpers when she thinks no one's listening. She has become a blade of bone.

"Happy," she says, "do you love me?"

For a crazy moment, I believe I can save her. I kiss her

hands. I kiss the knuckles and the scars. I kiss what used to be callused flesh.

"Did we kill her?" she asks.

"No," I say.

"Will she go to heaven?"

"Absolutely."

"Will we?"

"Pudge..."

"Will she forgive us?" Pudge asks.

No, I think, *never*. "Absolutely," I say.

"Why?"

"I don't know."

Mom calls. Staff pulls me from school and brings me to the nurses' station where Mom is waiting on the phone.

"Happy," Mom says.

"Mom."

"Jim called."

"Oh."

"Why?" she says. "You didn't...you should've called."

"I'm sorry."

"I want to be there."

"Me too."

"Happy, what happened?"

"I don't know. She came too early."

"Jesus."

"She's dying."

"No."

"She's too small." I listen to her swallow the tears. I listen to her breathe for a moment. "There's nothing we can do."

"Happy," she says, "are you okay?"

I shrug and remember she can't see it. I don't care.

"Happy?"

"I don't know what to do."

"It's okay."

"No, Mom. It's not."

"I'm sorry," she says. "I know."

"No, you don't." I can hear her smoking her cigarette. I can hear her doing something with her hands.

"I'll be there in a little bit," she says.

"Okay."

"I'm so sorry," she says.

"Me too."

"I'll see you in a bit."

"Okay."

Staff doesn't push me back to school. He gives me a cigarette and sends me to sit in the Commons Pudge is there. On the couch. Completely still. Every time I see her now, she appears smaller and smaller. Folded into herself like a closed book. She stares at the empty television. She doesn't notice when I ease in beside her. She stares at something only she can see. I stare at her. A muscle in her neck twitches. When I reach out to touch it, she jumps away.

"Don't," she says. "Please. Don't touch me."

"Sorry."

Her eyes sit sunk in darkness. Blood bubbles from a crack in her white lip. "Is it over?"

"What?"

"I'm so tired," she says. "I thought I knew what pain was."

"Maybe if you lay down."

She shakes her head, hard. "It hurt," she says. "For a long time, it hurt and there was nothing I could do about, and then she was here. The doctors…they put her on my belly. She was…she was so small. Blue. Babies aren't supposed to be blue. She didn't cry or move. She just lay there. I held her and then…and then they took her. I thought I knew what it meant to hurt. They took her." Pudge looks right at me then. "Don't ask me…don't tell me about her. I can't… if I hold on…physical pain ain't shit." Pulling her knees to her chin, she goes back to looking out the window. "Too many thoughts," she says. "When I close my eyes…do you know what it's like…do you…do you ever have trouble just stopping…trouble getting the thoughts…never mind."

"I don't know what to do," I say.

"Me either," she says. "I see things." She says presses her finger to the window. "I sit here and I see the world going on. Those trees." I follow the point of her finger. A line of poplars stands straight and stark in gray light. "They move when the wind blows. They dance a little in the rain."

"Okay."

"But then they stop," she says. "They stop and they wait… they're always there." Her eyes close. Her chest lifts a little. "I never gave much thought to things," she says. "You know? Trees. Grass. Stones…they're there now and they'll be there when we're gone. They're completely indifferent. They don't care…they haven't even noticed how bad things are…they do their thing and we suffer and they don't even bother to pay attention. It's…it's…it drives me a little crazy…and… and it scares me. A little." She shifts and winces. "I'm so tired." Then, something changes in her. She gets sharper. A little more focused. "You've seen her?"

"Yeah."

Pudge rests her hand on my knee. "You're a good boy," she says. "You would've been a good dad." I blush. All I can do is bite my lip. "She's lucky to have you."

"You can…"

Her hand comes up. Fingertips press against my mouth. "Don't."

"Sorry."

A sad smile. She turns back to the window and forgets I'm there.

Staff comes for me. "Happy," he says. "Your mom."

"Pudge," I say.

"Go on," she says with a small smile.

"I can…" I say. "Maybe Mom…"

"Sweetie," Pudge says, "go."

Another minute. But then I stand. Things seem to tear. "I'm sorry."

"Me too."

Mom stands with Jim at the nurses' station. When I walk up, she wraps her arms around me. "I'm so mad," she says.

"Mom."

"You should've called."

"I didn't know."

"Jesus," Mom says. "Don't you know…you can tell me anything."

"No," I say. "I can't."

Her tired face sags from too large bones. "Happy," she says.

"Can we go?" I ask. Jim wears his disapproval plain on his face. "Please."

Mom turns to Jim. The Door to the World buzzes. They follow me out to the hall.

Walking to the hospital seems to take too long. Having Mom with us adds a certain weight. Rain falls in a bitter mist. Leaves molder in the gutters. Cars carrying people we don't know go to places we don't care about.

"Maybe today," Mom says, "they'll have something good to say."

"Mrs. O'Neill," Jim says. "You need to know..."

"Do you believe in miracles, Doctor?" Mom asks.

"Yes, ma'am," he says, "I do."

"You told me you were praying for my son," she says.

"Yes, ma'am."

"Pray for my granddaughter then," she says. "Pray that God has mercy on a child who did nothing wrong...a child completely innocent..."

Something sharp catches in her throat. She presses her fingers to her mouth.

"Just pray, Jim," she says. "Please."

"Yes, ma'am."

The hospital is the hospital. I no longer notice the safe and pasty pastel landscapes hanging on the eggshell walls. People in scrubs disappear in the mix. Visitors, people in everything from suits to jeans, mill and wander. They gather in groups talking. Mom watches them and I watch her. Part of me, the part that finds threats in everything, wonders what she's thinking.

I know the way. Jim no longer has to lead. I plow ahead, anxious to get to the glass separating me from my daughter. When we get there, a man stands with a woman. Faces close enough to the glass to fog it a bit. The woman wears a long nightgown. An IV hangs from her arm. Tears well from bloodshot eyes. The man keeps a protective arm around her.

"It's okay," he keeps saying. "It'll be fine."

I want to yell at him.

"Which one?" Mom asks.

Jim shakes his head. I look through the glass. The crib holding my daughter is empty. A shock trembles through me. I check every crib for Bess's face. I look for her red hair. Nothing. Nurses move from baby to baby. I tap on the glass.

"What's happening?" Mom asks.

A nurse looks up. Her eyes go a little wide. She holds one finger and turns to another nurse who twitched. Not good. The first nurse disappears through a white door.

"Happy," Jim says.

"No."

"Happy, it's okay."

"No," I say. "No."

The doctor is neither young nor old. A white lab coat covers blue scrubs. "She died," the doctor says. The words make no sense. "We did what we could," the doctor says. "She was just too small."

"Dear God," Jim says.

Mom sniffs. "Can we see her?"

"Yes," the doctor says. "This way."

A tech takes us to the basement. Pale plaster gives way to white cinderblock. Windows vanish. Cold air pushes on us. I'm empty and full at the same time. I'm slick and rough. Walking in the hall, walking to the basement, I feel the earth around me. I'm surrounded with stone and metal and air.

Bess lies on a metal shelf. Her arms lay stretched out. Her legs bowed. She's blue and gray, the color of a robin's egg. Red hair. Her eyelids are swollen. Dark. Closed forever.

I touch her. I hold her. She weighs nothing. She's so small, she's almost not real. Somehow, she fades into memory and memory paints her so vividly; I have to swallow a scream. Somehow, she becomes a piece of something larger than the world. She becomes a wish.

I lay my daughter on the shelf. I lay my girl on shiny, cold metal and walk away. Mom wraps an arm around me. I push her away. I walk alone into the hall.

"Happy," Mom says. I wave her off. I walk. I stop. Violence storms through me. I punch the wall. Something in my hand snaps. I punch again. And again. I punch until Jim wraps me up and hauls me to the floor. Mom drops and hugs us both. "Stop," she says. "Please. Stop."

I don't want to. I want to break things. I want to hurt someone but Jim won't let go. Mom holds my face in her hands. Everything in me collapses into darkness and tears.

They give me a shot of something. Jim holds on. Mom stands over us.

"Happy," she says. "What're you doing?" I shake my head. Mostly, the fight's over. Still I jerk against Jim's arms now and then. "Stop," Mom says. "Just stop."

"Are you done?" Jim asks. Whatever they gave me takes hold. All the rage. All the sadness cuts away. It's still there but now it's in a box and stored somewhere for later. Words won't come. I let my body go slack. "I'm going to let you go," Jim says. "I want you to put your hands in your lap. Can you do that?" I nod. "Good."

Slowly, he let me go. Awkwardly, he gets to his feet. He grunts and stumbles around a little. I notice he's favoring one leg. Part of me feels bad. Part of me is proud. The old man may have won but he isn't walking without knowing he was in a fight. Jim stands next to Mom. He looks at her but she won't look at him. "Mrs. O'Neill," he says.

"Bet. Call me Bet."

"Bet," he says, "are you okay?" She nods but it's a lie. Even from the floor, I can see her face and it's held together simply by force of will. Still, Jim takes her at her word. He turns to me. He kneels and takes my hand. "Maybe broken," he says.

"Jesus, Hap," Mom says. "What's wrong with you?"

I shake my head.

We stop by the ER. They ask about my pain. I don't know how to answer. I can't separate the pain inside from the pain outside. The doctor shakes his head. Mom holds my other hand. Focusing on the immediateness of broken bones gives us all a little break. A little time to wrap things up in reality. They send me for an X-ray. I've broken my hand. They wrap it in a cast and send me back to C-Ward.

"Are we going to have trouble?" Jim asks. "Do I need to call anyone?"

"I'm fine," I say.

"Good," Jim says.

Everything blurs. Noise and motion. My body moves more from habit than choice. Mom walks with me but she keeps quiet. Jim keeps himself between me and the street. He knows what he's doing. He knows how to handle these things. Part of me gets it. Finally. He's human but he knows things. They might not be the right things but he knows them nonetheless.

We tell Pudge. Mom and Jim and me. Her room is still her room. Empty now. No photos. No poems. Just a bed with dull blankets. A small pile of clothes in the corner. She sits on her bed. Her face goes hard and still. "Dead?" she says, quietly.

"They did everything they could," Jim says.

Pudge blinks. "Dead." Mom reaches for her hand, but Pudge jerks away. "It's over."

"It's over," I say.

She looks at me. She's been waiting for this. "Okay." Jim stands. Mom doesn't move. "Okay," Pudge says again.

"Do you need anything?" Mom asks.

"Someone has to tell Ding," Pudge says. "Someone has to tell my mom."

"I can call her," Jim says.

"Okay.

Pudge rocks a little. She looks out the window. Somehow, she gets smaller. Younger. "What's next?" she asks. No one says anything. "Okay," Pudge says, looking at us. "I think I need to lie down for a while."

"I'm right here," I say, rising to my feet.

She waves a hand at me and turns her face to the wall. "Later," she says.

"Okay."

I turn to the door. Jim follows. Mom kneels down next to Pudge's bed and strokes her hair for a moment. She whispers something before standing.

Mom and I go to my room. She sits on the bed. I sit next to her. Not touching. My thoughts are mushy. They're soft and jagged at the same time. My thoughts lie in my head like mud and barbed wire. *I have a daughter*, I think. *My daughter's dead.*

Six days. Bess lived for six days. For six days, I was almost real. I was almost something bigger. For six days, I saw things unfolding, changing. Six days. For six days, I was almost human.

Mom wraps an arm around me. We're not physical people. The weight of her arm is massive. I slide onto the mattress. I wrap my arms around her middle. Mom strokes my hair. Gently. Softly. I cry. Wracking sobs. My chest hurts. My eyes burn. I feel sick and Mom holds me while the world spins on without me.

Mom goes home. Pudge stays in her room. Staff gives me cigarettes. I sit alone in the Commons. Not alone. People keep coming to me. "I'm sorry," they say, but none of them know what they're sorry for.

Night comes. The sky on the window's far side turns yellow and red and purple. The mountains stand ragged on the horizon. Blackbirds swirl in the distance. None of it matters. None of it cares one bit about my dead daughter.

"Happy," Staff says. "Are you okay?" I shake my head. "Jim wrote an order for you," she says. "Something to help with the pain." I look at her blankly. "For your hand," she says. "And something to help you sleep."

It's a distant kindness. It's Jim trying to ease me through the night. Staff brings me pills. I take them and wait. The night turns soft. Voices go quiet. The high helps. Everything backs off. If I hold still enough, long enough, maybe things will be fine.

I float on memories and the pills' gentle high. Jules comes and sits with me. She looks at me with her wide, weird eyes. "Does it hurt?" she asks. I look at her. "Dying. Does it hurt?"

"It hurt me."

"Sometimes," Jules says. "I pretend I'm already dead. There's no pain. There's just…there's just a heavy blackness."

"Jules."

"I'm sorry." She picks at a scar on her wrist. "I just…I'm sorry. My mom says that babies…there's a special place in heaven. She says they get to be gods."

"Please," I say.

"I just want you to know," Jules says, "your baby…your baby's going to be a god."

"Jules. Go away. Please."

❧

"She's dead," Pudge says.

"I know."

"I can't."

I take her hand and she pulls away. I take it again and she tries to pull away again. I hold tight. "We did this," I say. "You and me."

"No. She's dead, Happy."

"I know," I say. "You know what? You know what… you're the only one who got to hold her when she was alive. You got to feel her heart beat. I didn't. You're the only who knew what she was like when she was alive."

"Stop," Pudge says.

"We did this," I say.

Pudge shakes her head. Tears dribbled from her chin. "I can't."

"You got to hold her."

"Go away," she says.

"No."

Her hollow face looks right into mine. "Do you think she knows?" Pudge asks.

I shake my head. "Jim believes in heaven."

"Do you?"

"I don't know what I believe."

A long moment. "Was it horrible?" she asks, wanting me to let her off the hook. "Did we kill her?"

"No…I don't know."

"Do you think it'll ever get better?"

"No," I say. "It'll only get older."

Pudge wants me to tell her everything's going to be okay. She wants me to tell her we'd done nothing wrong. I can't do it. Pudge wants me to forgive her. She presses her head to my chest. She listens to my heart beat. She kisses me. A communion of sorts. A twisted Liturgy of the Flesh.

"Happy, please." I kiss her lips. I kiss her scars. I stroke her hair. "Is this the end?"

"A beginning maybe," I say.

"A beginning?"

"Never mind."

The next day, I come out of a bad dream and go to breakfast. Pudge no longer waits for me. I sit without eating. Staff no longer pushes me. They let me smoke. They leave me alone.

After breakfast, Staff rings their bell and we line up. They count us. No Pudge. I ask about it.

"She's gone," Staff says.

"Gone?"

"Her mom picked her up," Staff says. "Last night."

A coldness spread out from my chest to my fingers. "She went home? She just left?"

"Sorry."

"Jesus."

"Sorry."

Everything's empty. Everything's still. "Okay."

There's nothing left for me. Bug's gone. Vanished. Pudge's gone now too. Again, vanished. C-Ward is nothing but walls and people. Bess is dead. I'm done. Somehow, I talk Mom into bringing me home. She calls Jim and Jim tries to talk her out of it. He calls me into his office.

"It's a bad idea," Jim says. "You've just been through something."

"I know."

"I'm worried."

"Me too," I say.

His eyes narrow. "What do you want? I can help."

I shake my head. "I'm done."

"What's that mean?"

"It means I'm done."

"I don't like it," he says.

I shrug. He shakes his head.

The night before leaving, I don't sleep. I sit in the window of my room watching the rain break the light into rainbows on the glass. I watch the shadows of trees in the distance twitching black on black against the night. Occasionally, cars cast their headlights through the hedge at the edge of the lawn.

I try to shower but the water is too cool. All it does is make me wet and far too awake. Just before dawn, I ask Staff for a cigarette. He looks at me sideways but hands one over.

The window in the Commons face the wrong direction to catch the sunrise. Instead, it catches its reflection. The sky goes purple then slightly gray and finally, the sun rises high enough for full daylight to spread over the lawn.

People quietly trickle in. Mornings this early are simply not made for noise. Everyone moves with a certain caution, as if afraid of breaking something. When the Commons is mostly full, Staff brings in breakfast. I don't eat. It's time to get ready.

I spend awhile packing my things. Clothes. A few books. When that's done, I sit on the edge of my bed and wait, getting more and more anxious. I'm ready to go, but C-Ward isn't ready to let me go.

When Mom finally arrives, Staff comes for me. I only have one bag. Mostly, I carry memories. I look around wondering how long it'll be before I forget about this place and all the shit that came with it.

"Ready?" Mom asks. She carries my bag. An unnecessary kindness. In the car, I grab a cigarette and light up. Mom looks at me. "You okay?"

"Yeah."

The city gives way to mountains. The trees grow taller and thick on the ground. Naked oaks. Elms. Evergreens catch the clouds, stretching them into long, tattered strings. Buildings turn from concrete and glass to wood and brick. Businesses become farms. Fields of clover and winter wheat, pastures hold sheep and horses and cattle. We drive west. Into the mountains. Toward the ocean. Toward home.

The box sits on the coffee table. Too small. Too white. Too plain. I decide this is what sadness looks like. Simple and hard edged. It's hard to believe the thing holds Bess's ashes.

A life should be bigger, I think, but the box is no bigger than a shoe box.

"What're you going to do?" Mom asks.

"I don't know."

"No rush."

"No," I say. "It's not like she's waiting."

Mom goes to work. Mom always goes to work. Before she

leaves, she takes my face in her hands. "I'm trusting you," she says.

"I know."

She kisses my cheek. "You stay safe."

"Mom."

"I'm worried."

"I'm fine."

She tilts her head. "Good," she says but she doesn't sound like she believes me.

I take Bess's ashes through town. I walk to the bridge over the creek running at the edge of things. This is where Dad used to take me when I was a kid. We killed fish here. That's what Dad called it. "Fishing is passive," he used to say. "We are not passive. We're here to kill fish." This is where we spread his ashes.

The water is white, gurgling over a stack of stones. The bank is steep and muddy and cold. I slide down to the water, careful not to drop the box. I stand for a long time. When I take my shoes off, the cold mud squishes up around my toes, giving me a bit of a shiver. I wade in until the water reaches my waist. It's cold, sharp as a blade. Starlings slice the sky to ribbons. Bess's ashes are fine, silky to touch. It's hard to believe that this dust is all that's left of my daughter. It's hard to believe this gray mist rising in the wind was once a baby.

I pour it all into the water, and a small cloud rises into the wind. I imagine Bess flying over the trees. I imagine my daughter covering the world.

CPSIA information can be obtained
at www.ICGtesting.com
Printed in the USA
FFHW02n2136270818
48035632-51763FF